A Place For Margaret

The Margaret Trilogy
A Place for Margaret
Margaret in the Middle
Margaret on her Way

BERNICE THURMAN HUNTER

A Place For Margaret

Cover photo by Rick Buncombe

Scholastic Canada Ltd.

Scholastic Canada Ltd.
123 Newkirk Road, Richmond Hill, Ontario, Canada L4C 3G5

Scholastic Inc.
730 Broadway, New York, NY 10003, USA

Ashton Scholastic Limited
Private Bag 1, Penrose, Auckland, New Zealand

Ashton Scholastic Pty Limited
PO Box 579, Gosford, NSW 2250, Australia

Scholastic Publications Ltd.
Holly Walk, Leamington Spa, Warwickshire CV32 4LS, England

Grateful thanks to Hewson Clydesdales, Petra Hewson, and "Timmy."

Canadian Cataloguing in Publication Data

Hunter, Bernice Thurman
    A place for Margaret

ISBN 0-590-73665-5

I. Title.

PS8565.U577P54 1984   jC813'.54   C84-099393-5
PZ7.H86P1 1984

11 10 9 8 7 6   Printed in Canada   0 1 2 3 4 5/9
Manufactured by Webcom Limited

For Anita Louise and Heather Anne

Contents

1
Starr

The first time we met he bit me. I held out my hand, straight and flat, just like Aunt Margaret said, but Starr snapped at it so excitedly with his big yellow teeth that he nipped my skin and made it bleed. It hurt like the dickens and I yelled blue murder, scaring the wits out of him. Then he turned tail and galloped across the meadow, disappearing into the woods on the other side.

The next time was just as bad. I was lying in the hammock feeling sorry for myself and missing the city noises. I wasn't used to the quiet of the country, where all you ever heard were bees and bugs and the odd cow mooing. My home in Toronto was on Jones Avenue right near Gerrard Street, where the air practically vibrated with the clanging of trolley cars, the squealing of sirens and the racket of a hundred screaming kids.

So at first I spent a lot of my time on the farm lying around pining for home. I did this in the hammock that Uncle Herb had slung between two poles in the front yard especially for me. There were lots of trees he could have slung it from but Aunt Marg said I wouldn't get enough sunshine under them. "Of all God's miracles," she said, and she could name them off by the peck, "sunshine is far and away the best. It cures nearly anything that ails you." Anything except loneliness, I thought dejectedly.

That day, as I was lazing in the sun talking to my imaginary friend, Emily (I had invented Emily so I wouldn't go crazy), I suddenly had this creepy feeling come over me that somebody was watching me. I swivelled my eyes around nervously, and there was Starr with his big brown head lolling over the fence staring straight at me.

We eyed each other curiously. I don't know what he thought of me, but I thought he was beautiful. He was chestnut brown with a white star the length of his nose, a thick tawny mane and the most peculiar long white eyelashes I'd ever seen on a horse. He batted them at me now, sweeping them down over his shiny dark eyes, which just happened to be the same colour as my own.

I got out of the hammock the quickest way I knew how, by rolling over and landing kerplunk on the ground. Startled, he flung up his head, gave a piercing whinny and went tearing across the field as if the devil himself were after him.

"What did you do to him?" called Aunt Marg from the porch. She set down the two pails of milk she was carrying and threw her floppy straw hat up on a nail.

"Nothing!" I pouted, close to tears. "He just doesn't like me, I guess."

"Well, never you mind," she laughed, holding the door open with her backside and lifting the pails into the kitchen. "I like you!" The door clacked shut behind her.

I already knew that! But I wanted Starr to like me. So the next time he hung his head over the fence I was ready for him. Instead of being in the hammock, I was sitting stock-still on the little bench that I had dragged down from the porch — the one Aunt Marg set her bread tins out on. Rising slowly to my feet, I tiptoed towards him, carefully balancing two sugar cubes on the end of a long, flat stick. But as soon as I got close to him he bolted.

"Dang!" I swore, throwing the stick at the fence. "Not even a *horse* will come near me!"

* * *

Boy, I was lonely those first weeks on Uncle Herb's farm. Every night I'd say to Aunt Margaret, "I want to go home." And she'd say, "But Margaret" — I was named after her —"if you go home the doctor will send you to the TB sanitarium. You don't want that, now do you?" And I'd say, "No, but at least at the sanitarium there might be other sick kids to play with."

That's why I had been sent to the farm. Because the doctor said I had TB, which is short for tuberculosis, and I had to be isolated. "It's either the san or the farm," he said, "take your pick." So my mother picked the farm.

In that summer of 1925, sunshine, home-cooking and good nursing care were all that could be done for TB. My mother said I was bound to get plenty of all three on the farm. "My sister Margaret is the best practical nurse in Ontario. Maybe in the whole country," she declared proudly. "Why, she's nursed hundreds of sick folk back to health after the doctors had given them up for lost. And she's only buried half a dozen so far."

"How long will I be gone, Ma?" I was beginning to get suspicious. What if I was dying and they weren't telling me?

"Oh, just a few weeks at the most, Peg." That's what I got called at home — Peg or Peggy. I didn't like either one. "Don't worry your head. Margaret will have you fit as a fiddle in no time at all."

Next came the problem of how to get me there. The farm was sixty-odd miles from Toronto, and my father didn't own a car. And I was too weak to travel by train. So the doctor volunteered to deliver me himself. He said his folks lived in Shelburne, which was the nearest town to Uncle Herb's farm, and he owed them a visit.

So Ma packed my grip and slipped a snapshot of our whole family into the side pocket. "Just so you don't forget us," she said.

Then the doctor bundled me in a woollen rug and laid me out on the back seat of his Pierce Arrow. It had a lovely new-car smell and I would have enjoyed the trip if I'd been feeling better. On the other hand, if I'd been feeling better I wouldn't have got to go. So it was six of one and half a dozen of the other.

Curled up on the velvety seat, I soon fell fast asleep. The next thing I knew the doctor was calling, "Wake up, missy. We're here!"

I jumped up, rubbing my eyes, and stared out the front window as he steered the Arrow up the long lane leading to the green farmhouse. At least it used to be green, but now the paint was flaking off, letting the parched grey wood show through. A weather-beaten sign nailed to the fencepost read, in faded letters, *Green Meadows*.

My aunt and uncle were both on the porch to greet us. Uncle Herb was a solid looking man, with wiry red hair, a friendly grin that showed the space between his teeth, and a farmer's burnt complexion. He had on grey overalls and a blue-checkered shirt. Aunt Marg was a stockily-built woman in a house-dress that looked as if it had been cut from the same cloth as Uncle Herb's shirt. She had red hair coiled up in a bun, fair freckly skin and a wide sweet smile. They looked almost like twins.

The first thing I said was, "Am I going to die?"

Uncle Herb let out a hoot of laughter and the straw he had been wiggling between his teeth flew out of his mouth. "You do and your aunt will kill you!" he cried.

That made us all laugh. Then the doctor assured me that I was going to get well, and my aunt and uncle thanked him for dropping me off (like a sack of potatoes, joked Uncle Herb). I was soon tucked in under an afghan on the day-bed in the big farm kitchen.

I liked the kitchen. It was a homey room with a huge black iron stove, a long wooden table and six plain chairs. A washstand stood by the door with a graniteware basin on top and a pail of water underneath. The floor was made of wide boards with no linoleum. At the end of the room was a door that led upstairs to the bedrooms.

Both my aunt and uncle were nice, which in my experience is pretty unusual. Most often if your aunt is nice your uncle is awful — or vice versa.

* * *

Aunt Marg worried a lot about my loneliness because she said that pining would hinder my progress. But since I wasn't allowed within a mile of other people, especially children, what could she do?

Of course she spent as much time with me as she could spare. Every night before bed she'd play a game of dominoes with me or read me a story when the TB made me too tired to read to myself.

But because it was the haying season and Uncle Herb didn't have a hired hand, Aunt Marg had to help out. So she had to leave me on my own more than she really liked.

It was a small farm, with just one horse — Starr, two cows — Flora and Fauna, and a flock of black and white hens that Aunt Marg called her "ladies." They didn't have regular names like the other livestock. Uncle Herb said his farm was a one-man operation.

"One man and one woman!" Aunt Marg reminded him dryly.

"You're right there, Mag." That's what he called her sometimes — Mag. She didn't like it because it rhymed with hag, but there was no use trying to stop him. "That man!" she wagged her finger in his direction. "That uncle of yours. Why, if I didn't love him so much I'd have sent him packing long ago!"

* * *

The second week I was there it rained cats and dogs so I had to stay indoors and rest on the day-bed, with only my imaginary friend, Emily, for company. Sometimes I heard Starr neighing in the distance, which only made me feel more lonely.

Then one day Uncle Herb came in sopping wet; he slapped his hat on his knee and showered me with raindrops as he handed me a letter. I recognized the writing instantly. It was from my sister Josie, the one I was the closest to and shared the bed with at home. Squealing with delight, I ripped it open.

June 16, 1925.

Dear Peg,

How are you? I hope you are lots better. We're all fine down here. We are having a swell summer so far. Do you know what we did last Saturday? We had a block picnic and all the families on our block went to High Park. All the mothers packed lunch baskets. Ma made egg and bologna sandwiches and gumdrop cake.

There must have been a hundred people there altogether. Even Olive and Elmer went. (Olive and Elmer were the oldest in our family and they usually thought they were too grown-up to go on family outings.) The minute we jumped off the trolley car we all trooped down to where the animals are kept and fed them carrot tops through the fence. Then we played games like Shadow Tag and Cowboys and Indians. That's lots of fun in High Park because there are so many big trees to hide behind. The big boys played Buck, Buck, How Many Fingers Up? Our Harry was at the bottom of the heap and he nearly got his back broke when fat Theodore Duncan landed on top of him. So Jenny begged him to quit. (Jenny was Harry's twin so they were extra close.) Gracie and Davey were good as gold and didn't fight once because they were having so much fun playing London Bridges and Here I Sit A-Sewing. Bobby wet his drawers once so Ma put him back in napkins, but she didn't spank him. Flossie Gilmore went with Zelma Speares because Mrs. Gilmore had the vapours and couldn't go. (Flossie Gilmore was my best friend, but who the heck was Zelma Speares?)

At suppertime the men put the picnic tables in rows, end to end, so we could all sit down together. There was tons of food and oceans of lemonade. Afterwards we kids layed around on the grass moaning and holding our stomachs. Then we started telling jokes and stories.

When the women got the tables all cleared

up and the men came back from their walk, the grownups played progressive euchre. The big kids, like Olive and Elmer, were allowed to play too.

On our way home on the trolley car we flipped the wicker seatbacks over so we could ride facing each other. Then everybody sang "Hail, hail, the gang's all here, what the heck do we care, long as we got our carfare" and after that we sang "Show me the way to go home, over land or sea or foam." It was the most fun I ever had in my life. Even better than kids' day at the Ex and the rides at Sunnyside. Too bad you missed it.

I was so tired when I got home I went to bed without washing myself and Ma didn't even notice. I really like sleeping alone. There's no one to poke me when I wiggle my toes, and make me shove over. And it doesn't matter that the bed sinks down in the middle when there's only one person in it. But I miss you quite a bit, Peg, and hope you miss me too. Goodbye. Write soon.

Your sister, Josie.

P.S. Ma and Pa want to add a line.

Hello there, daughter. I hope you're being a good girl and not giving any trouble. And I hope this finds you well. Write me a note when you feel up to it. I'll hand the pen to your Pa now.

Your loving mother.

Well, Peg, we received your aunt's welcome letter a day or two ago saying how much better you are. That's sure good news to us. We'll be looking for you home at the end of the summer.

Lovingly, your father.

That night I went to bed early, but I didn't blow out the lamp right away. Instead, I got the picture of my family down off the washstand mirror and studied it for a long time. We all looked so happy standing in a bunch on the steps of our house on Jones Avenue. I noticed every little thing — the welcome mat hanging crooked over the railing, Bobby's damp drawers drooping down, our old Flyer wagon lying on its side on the weedy lawn. I remembered what fun it was coasting down the hill on Jones Avenue. I stared hard at each face, especially Ma's and Pa's, hoping I could make myself dream about them.

Josie's letter had made me feel better and worse both at once. I was glad to hear all the news from home, but how come, I wondered, they never thought of having a block picnic before, then all of a sudden when I'm not there, they have one?

I sighed and stuck the snapshot back up on the looking glass. Then I spread-eagled myself on the bed. It *was* nice having a bed to myself. And my own room, too! At home there were two beds in each room and two kids to a bed. My bed on the farm was a double one that didn't sink in the middle. And it was extra soft because it had a downy feather tick. And Emily never wiggled her toes and she didn't take up any space at all.

Now, if only I could win over that stubborn horse!

2
The secret signal

Three more days passed before it was dry enough to go outside. Then I decided to get up the nerve to stand on Starr's side of the fence. Uncle Herb had just taken the bit out of his mouth and turned him loose after a hard day's work. He hadn't had his water yet and froth bubbled around his muzzle.

When he spotted me he stopped short and stood perfectly still, blinking with those long white eyelashes. He pawed the ground, tossing his head, then, ever so slowly, came ambling towards me. Suddenly I realized how huge an animal he was. With all my might I willed my hand to stay steady and my heart to stop its thumping. I held a big red apple out at arm's length on my sweaty palm. It must have looked refreshing, because he stepped right up and took it — *crunch!* — and the juice sprayed out and clung in sparkling beads to his whiskers.

Just then Uncle Herb opened the gate and came staggering over with a tub of freshly pumped well-water. He set it down with a grunt and a splash and

11

Starr plunged his nose right in up to his snowy lashes.

"What are you doing here, youngster?" asked Uncle Herb, mopping his brow with his sleeve. "I thought you were afraid of Starr." Turning his head he spat an arc of tobacco juice over his shoulder.

"No. I never was. He was afraid of me. But he's not now. He took an apple right off my hand without biting. See?" I proudly displayed my uninjured palm.

"Well, by rights you shouldn't make friends with work animals, Maggie." That's what he had been calling me lately. "They aren't pets, you know. Why don't you go play with Mabel?"

Mabel was the cat. A mean old mouser.

"Eww!" I wrinkled my nose. "I don't like her. She's nasty and she's got spots all over her."

"*Hah!*" He let out a big guffaw. "That sounds like the pot calling the kettle black." He walked away, chuckling to himself at his own joke.

I knew he was only teasing. Uncle Herb wasn't the type to go around hurting other people's feelings. Aunt Marg always said he didn't have a mean bone in his body. But just the same it bothered me because I was extra sensitive about my looks. I had big brown freckles splattered all over my face and arms, and I had to wear thick, steel-rimmed spectacles for my nearsightedness. Then, to top it off, my black hair, which used to be curly before I took sick, had gone all straight and stringy. So Uncle Herb's little joke didn't set too well with me. And his disapproval of my friendship with Starr brought out my stubborn streak and made me all the more determined. But after that I made sure he was nowhere in sight when I was wheedling Starr with treats.

Little by little the horse came to trust me. Every day he let me get a step nearer, until one day he allowed me to stroke the star on his nose for about fifteen minutes. After that it was as easy as falling off a log (or out of a hammock). I'd walk along beside him through the tall grass patting his smooth brown belly and talking to him a mile a minute. And when he leaned down to munch a patch of sweet clover, I'd fling my arms around his broad neck and give him a huge hug. Then, when he raised his handsome head, I'd kiss him right on the lips. His muzzle was soft and warm, like a hairy velvet pillow.

The secret signal happened by accident. One day I saw Starr grazing on the other side of the meadow. He was so far away he looked no bigger than an ant. I thought he wouldn't hear me if I called his name, so I decided to whistle. I pursed my lips and curled my tongue and blew and blew and blew. I nearly blew my head off but no sound came — just air. Then the strangest thing happened. Starr raised his head and stared in my direction. It seemed that he had heard my soundless whistle ... or felt it ... or sensed it ... or something.

Anyhow, after that, no matter where he was, when I blew he'd stop whatever he was doing, throw up his head, spot me and come galloping towards me, his tawny mane waving like wheat in the wind, his tail flying like a banner.

It was swell having a horse for a friend ... and I wasn't nearly so lonely any more.

3
My dilemma

I had been on the farm for three whole months — June, July and August — when Doctor Tom (we called him by his first name because he and Uncle Herb had been boys together) announced that I was cured.

All summer long, whenever he was passing by in his horse and buggy (he said one of these fine days he was going to get himself a car), he'd stop in to take a look at me. Then at the end of August he gave me a thorough going over.

Aunt Marg stood anxiously by as he listened with his stethoscope, told me to cough, thumped me on the back and pronounced me sound as a dollar. "But just to be on the safe side," he said, snapping shut his black leather bag, "it wouldn't hurt if she stayed up here in the country for another month, or as long as the good weather lasts."

"Well, Margaret," Aunt Marg gave me a searching look, "what do you think? Do you want to stay a while longer? It's up to you, girl, because as far as your uncle and I are concerned you're as welcome as the flowers in May."

I didn't know what to say because I was taken by surprise. It suddenly got quiet in the kitchen. The only sounds were the ticking of the clock on the wall and the noise of a giant blowfly banging on the window.

If I stayed it would mean I'd be late starting school. I didn't mind that because I was smart. I knew it would be easy to catch up. (I always reasoned that God had given me extra brains to make up for my homeliness. Personally I'd have been satisfied with a little less of each.) Anyway, missing school didn't bother me, but missing my family did.

Every night I'd look at the snapshot stuck up on the mirror and "God bless" everybody. Josie had written me two more letters since the one about the picnic. And Ma and Pa each wrote me once telling me to behave myself and sending me a shinplaster to spend. But it wasn't the same as seeing them in person. Of course I knew they wouldn't miss me as much as I missed them because they had each other. There were nine kids in our family and I was the one in the middle. Sometimes I actually felt invisible. And I was perfectly at home with my aunt and uncle now.

For some reason that I hadn't gotten to the bottom of, they had no children of their own, so they treated me just as if I was theirs. Aunt Marg hugged me a lot and called me her "old sweetheart," even though I was only eleven, and Uncle Herb said I was a "corker." That's because I played tricks on him every chance I got. And being the only child in the house had its advantages. For one thing, I sure didn't feel invisible anymore.

All of a sudden my thoughts were interrupted by a high-pitched whinny from the paddock. "Excuse me!" I cried. "I think Starr's calling me." Then I bolted out the door.

Climbing the split-rail fence, I sat on the top rail and took Starr's smooth brown muzzle between my hands. I told him all about my dilemma, while he stared solemnly at me. Uncle Herb always said Starr couldn't understand long conversations, just short commands, but I disagreed. "What do you say, boy? Should I stay a while longer?"

He blinked his long white eyelashes thoughtfully. Then he nodded, the way horses do, swaying his head up and down.

"Thanks, boy!"

Jumping down, I ran straight back into the house. "Guess what?" I cried ecstatically. "Starr wants me to stay!"

"Well, for mercy sakes, so do I!" Aunt Marg grabbed me and hugged me so hard it hurt. "I'll get a letter off to your mother this very minute." Immediately she got the paper, pen and ink pot down from the shelf. And Doctor Tom offered to wait while she wrote it so he could drop it off at the Post Office.

* * *

By this time Uncle Herb had accepted the fact that Starr and I were a twosome. He said he didn't object just so long as I never interfered while they were working. Aunt Marg even credited the horse with helping to save my life. She said the minute I stopped pining I started on the mend. And she said next to God's good sunshine, Starr was my best medicine.

Aunt Marg was a special kind of grownup, the kind a child could really talk to. And now that the hay was all piled safely in the barn she had time to listen. Uncle Herb was a good listener too, so I told them just about everything. Almost. The one thing I didn't tell them about was my secret signal, the soundless whistle that only Starr could hear. I thought they might think I was imagining things (the way I imagined Emily; I had to stop talking to Emily because it gave Aunt Marg the heebie-jeebies) or that I was just being silly. Sometimes grownups, even nice ones, think that way. So I kept that to myself. Besides, it was fun having a secret with a horse.

Whenever Starr was free in the field I'd purse my lips and blow, and he'd come to me at a gallop, stopping in a shower of grass just inches from my toes.

I rode him bareback and combed his tangled mane and brushed his smooth brown coat until it shone like a polished chestnut. I even tried to clean his teeth once with Aunt Marg's scrubbing brush, but he wouldn't keep his lips folded back long enough for me to get the job done.

One day, after catching my signal with those long, pointy ears of his, he came limping, instead of running, across the meadow. I nearly had a fit.

"What's the matter, boy?" I cried in alarm.

Lifting the hairy hoof he was favouring (his

hooves were shaggy and tawny coloured, matching his tail and mane), I saw that there was a sharp stone wedged between his flesh and the shoe.

"You wait here, boy," I said. "I'll be right back."

I ran to the house, got a knife from the kitchen table drawer, and ran back as fast as my legs would go.

I rested his injured hoof between my knees, in the hammock of my dress, and dug out the stone as gently as possible. His hoof began to bleed, so I washed it with soap and water and doused it with a whole bottle of peroxide. When the peroxide stopped fizzing I knew the wound was purified. And the bleeding stopped too. Through it all my brave stallion hadn't even flinched.

"Good boy, Starr!" I rewarded him with a kiss on the flat of his nose. "Does that feel better?"

In answer, he flung up his head, kicked up his heels and went tearing around in circles with hardly a sign of a limp.

"Nice work, Maggie!" Uncle Herb complimented me when I told them all about it at the supper table. "You're a natural with animals. I think you should be a vet when you grow up."

"Your uncle's right," Aunt Marg agreed, placing a hot slice of huckleberry pie, topped with clotted cream, in front of me. "You seem to have an affinity for God's creatures, Margaret. I've even noticed my ladies following after you."

"What's an affinity?" I asked, scooping up the cream which had juicy blue rivers wending through it.

18

"It means a special understanding," she explained. "Animals sense they can trust you more than most folks."

It wasn't long after that that my affinity was put to a real test.

4
Fire!

One night in the middle of September we were wakened by a horrendous storm. A huge thunderclap shook the frame farmhouse from top to bottom and jogged us all out of our beds. We ran downstairs and Aunt Marg lit the biggest oil lamp.

Great bolts of lightning flashed across the sky and lit up the whole world as plain as day.

"That was close." Uncle Herb was standing in his nightshirt at the open door. Then he added, "Ain't it eerie how quiet it gets in between?"

"Get away from there, you foolish man!" Aunt Marg yanked him back by the shirt tail. "Sometimes, Herb Wilkinson, you've got no more sense than a dewworm. And don't say 'ain't'!" she added for good measure.

No sooner had she spoken than another charge, ten times brighter than the last, zigzagged earthward and struck the barn dead centre.

"The animals!" cried Uncle Herb, and without hesitating for a second, he raced towards the barn, his shirt tail flying. Aunt Marg ran after him. And I ran after Aunt Marg. Suddenly the rain began.

"Go back, Margaret!" Aunt Marg screeched over her shoulder, "You'll catch your death!"

But the cloudburst had come too late to save the barn. Orange flames were already shooting skyward from the hayloft. And the stable was attached to the barn. And Starr was in the stable!

"*Starr! Starr! Starr!*" I screamed and kept on coming.

Uncle Herb ran straight into the smoke-filled barn and disappeared from sight. Then, one by one, he dragged the terrified, bellowing cows out by their horns. Aunt Marg grabbed up a switch and drove them into the safety of the paddock. Meanwhile, Uncle Herb had gone back inside for Starr.

Suddenly I was sobbing and crying out loud, "Oh, God, please don't let Starr die! Please save my horse."

Aunt Marg put her arms around me and sheltered me in her flannel kimono. The rain streamed down and the lightning flashed all around us. But we were oblivious to the danger. "Save my man, dear Lord," I heard Aunt Marg pray, "save my man." Her long red hair, which she had let down for the night, whipped around us like wet rope, plastering us together.

Our eyes were glued to the barn door. Smoke poured out, and over the noise of the cracking thunder and teeming rain, we could hear Starr's terror-filled cries.

"I'm going in there," declared Aunt Marg, just as Uncle Herb came staggering out.

21

"He's panicked," Uncle Herb coughed and gasped, his face as black as a coalman's. "I can't get him out, even with a blanket over his head."

"I can do it!" I yelled. Then, before they could stop me, I broke free from my aunt's embrace and raced towards the barn.

"*Margaret! Margaret!*" I heard them cry above the tumult.

Through the doorway, all I could see was billowing black smoke and a wave of red flames. Turning my head to one side, I gulped my lungs full of fresh, rain-washed air. Then, closing my eyes tight, I stuck my head inside. It was like sticking my head in a furnace. Pursing my lips and curling my tongue, I blew with all my might.

Just as I was about to run out of breath, Starr — poor, wild, terrified beast — came stumbling through the doorway.

The end of his tail was afire, but the rain put it out instantly. Round and round the barnyard he galloped in total panic. Thank goodness Uncle Herb had the presence of mind to shut the barn door so the horse, in his frenzy, wouldn't gallop right back into the inferno.

At last he tired and slowed to a walk. Finally he stopped, snorting and whimpering and pawing the ground. Then he saw me. Slowly he came to me and nuzzled his head in my arms. "*Starr*! Starr! There now, boy. Everything's going to be all right." I stroked his quivering muzzle soothingly.

His tail and mane were burned and bedraggled. And his long white eyelashes were all singed off. But he was safe, my friend Starr.

* * *

Uncle Herb was still shaking his head in bewilderment long after the animals were safely sheltered and the fire was out and we were sitting around the table, dry and warm, sipping mugs of hot cocoa.

"I still don't believe what I saw with my own eyes," he blinked. "Tell me again, Maggie, what you mean by your secret signal."

"Well, that's all there is to it, Uncle Herb, what I told you. I tried to whistle for Starr so I could call when he was out of earshot. But no matter how hard I blew I just couldn't make a whistle. But Starr seemed to hear anyway. No matter how far away he was. I can't explain it any better."

"Well, I said it before and I'll say it again — you're a corker, Maggie. A dad-blamed, solid-gold corker."

"The Lord works in strange ways," Aunt Marg remarked, feeling my forehead for the umpteenth time. She always thought the Lord planned things out ahead of time. And who knows, maybe she was right. Because if I had gone home, the storm would have come and the barn would have burned, and Starr would have perished for sure.

"It was meant to be, Margaret. It was destiny."

"Maybe I really do have an affinity."

"I'll drink to both them things," laughed Uncle Herb. Then he downed his hot cocoa in one gulp, wiped his chin with his clean nightshirt and poured himself another mug.

5
The barn raising

The barn was levelled to the ground. The next day, in spite of the torrential rains, it was still smouldering.

Starr and the cows were tethered temporarily in the driving shed along with the buggy and the cutter. The fire hadn't reached the shed or the hen house, so Aunt Marg's ladies were safe and sound.

They fluttered around us now as we came to gather eggs. "Come, my ladies!" Aunt Marg called to them politely. She never squawked, "Chook! Chook! Chook!" like other people did. With a wide swoop of her hand, she scattered grain from the folds of her apron.

"What's Uncle Herb going to do?" I worried, surveying, in dismay, the heap of steaming grey ash that used to be the barn.

"Oh, he'll have plenty of help rebuilding, never you fear. We'll have a new barn on that very spot before this week is out. And it'll mean lots of work for you and me, old sweetheart."

She wasn't just fooling. The barn raising was

scheduled for Saturday, and this was Monday, so after the wash was hung out we started into the baking. Hundreds of suet pies, baking-powder biscuits, raisin scones and seed cakes — enough to feed an army.

"Lucky my ladies are being so generous this week," remarked my aunt as she cracked a dozen eggs into a huge mixing bowl.

I must have filled a hundred tart shells with vanilla pudding. Then I stirred a big bowl of batter and poured it, without spilling any, into four huge, round cake tins with scrapers attached. When the cakes were cool all you had to do was twirl the scrapers around twice and the cakes came out clean as a whistle. Next Aunt Marg showed me how to make the icing.

"Are you getting tired, Margaret?" she looked at me anxiously. "You've been working like a Trojan this week, and after that soaking the night of the fire it'll be a mercy if you don't take a relapse."

"What the heck's a relapse?" I asked, licking chocolate icing off my fingers.

"It means the sickness might come back on you," she explained, leaning down to touch my forehead with her cheek, which was so flushed from the wood-stove fire that my forehead was bound to feel cold by comparison.

"Well, you don't need to worry, cause I never felt better in my life. I'm even getting fat." I patted my aproned stomach, leaving sticky brown prints on it.

Then something occurred to me.

"I guess that means I'll be going home soon."

The smile slid off Aunt Marg's face. "I hate to think what this house will be like without you, girl. You're just the best company that ever was. Why, you're my old sweetheart!" She stopped kneading a pile of dough just long enough to give me a floury hug. "And your Uncle Herb will be lost without your tricks. I thought he'd split his overalls laughing at the last one."

Just for fun, the day before, I had covered his red jelly dessert with cellophane. I tucked the clear paper under the wobbly mound so neatly that he couldn't even see it. Well, when he went to eat it, his spoon kept sliding off. "This gol-dang stuff is tough as shoe leather," he complained, giving it a hard poke. "What's it made of anyway, Mag?"

Aunt Marg got up, stone-faced, to make the tea. But I couldn't control myself. I giggled and snickered until I gave myself away. "You're a corker, Maggie," Uncle Herb said, giving my nose a tweak, "a genuine eighteen carat gold corker."

I tried to think up a new trick to play on him almost every day of the week. He had such a swell sense of humour. And he always made me feel good about myself by insisting that when the Lord made me he threw away the mould. "Leastways, I hope he did," he would add, "because another one like you would be the end of me."

Remembering this, I said to Aunt Marg, "Let's not talk about me leaving, at least until after the barn raising."

"Good idea," agreed my aunt, her round face brightening up, "Sufficient unto the day — "

"What's that mean?" She was always quoting mysterious things, mostly from the Bible.

"No time to explain. I've got to get this baking done before that uncle of yours wants his supper. I swear — you'd think that man's stomach was a clock, the way he tells the time by it."

She put four more raisin loaves into the hot oven, and we dropped the subject of my leaving for the time being.

On Saturday morning, while the rooster was still crowing, people began to arrive in droves: women and children and men ... horses and wagons and lumber ... saws and hammers and nails ... and more food!

I was beside myself with excitement. I hadn't seen another kid in months. So I ran out to meet a skinny fair-haired boy who was carrying a covered tray across the verandah. "Hi!" I cried. "My name's Margaret. What's yours?"

"My name's Matty — short for Matthew — but my ma said I had to stay clear of you because you're germy." As he spoke he started backing away towards the verandah steps.

"*Germy!*" Boy, did I see red! "How the heck can I be germy when Doctor Tom says I'm all better? Does your ma know more than Doctor Tom?"

"What's this ruckus all about?" demanded Aunt Marg from the doorway.

"He says I'm germy!" I howled indignantly. Then, before she could settle it one way or another, I took a flying leap at Matty and blew my breath all over his startled face.

"*Halp! Ma! I'm poisoned!*" He stumbled backwards off the top step. The tray flew up in the air, raining sandwiches all over the place like leaves on a windy day.

"*Margaret, go to your room!*" ordered my aunt.

"But Aunt Marg, I'm all better now and he said — "

"Go, Margaret!" She pointed to the stairs with the maddest look I'd ever seen on her face.

By this time Matty's mother got wind of it and she dragged him, wailing all the way, over to the well. Shoving his head under the spout, she pumped ice-cold water all over him.

Peeking out from the bottom step of the stairs, I heard Aunt Marg yell, "*Now you listen to me, Jessie Muggins*! That girl is no more germy than I am. And I'll get a doctor's certificate to prove it! And stop dousing that boy! What are you trying to do, drown him, or give him pneumonia? Cold water won't wash off germs even if there were any, you silly article!"

Now Mrs. Muggins hauled Matty into the kitchen, and without so much as a by-your-leave, grabbed our towel and began rubbing his head furiously.

Suddenly, for some devilish reason, I jumped into full view and shouted, "*You silly article!*" Then I jumped out of sight again. Halfway up the stairs I was sent sprawling by a hard smack on my behind. I turned around and came face to face with my aunt's flashing green eyes and flaming cheeks.

"Don't you dare let me hear you sass your elders like that again, you hear me? Now get!"

I high-tailed it up the rest of the way and slammed my bedroom door. When Aunt Marg came up, about fifteen minutes later, my backside was still smarting and my grip was all packed.

She sighed as she sat down, and the little wooden bed creaked under her weight. Shoving the grip over, she pulled me down beside her. "Margaret ... I'm sorry, my love, for striking you, especially since you're not my own. But it was the only thing I could think to do at the time."

"Uncle Herb wouldn't have hit me," I said defiantly.

Cupping my chin firmly in her hand, she made me face her. "Oh, yes he would, my girl. On important matters we see eye to eye, him and me."

I didn't dare answer back.

"Now, Margaret, there's something you need to know. Then, if you're still bent on going" — she glanced at the grip gaping open, a stocking hanging out, the family snapshot on top of my jumble of things — "I'll not stand in your way."

I waited for her to compose herself. I'd never seen her so agitated before, and I felt awful knowing I had caused it.

"Matty's mother, Jessie Muggins, was Jessie Hopkins before she wed. We were best friends when we were girls, and still are. At least I hope we are after this." I hung my head and noticed her hands twisting nervously on her lap. "Well, Jessie had a twin brother, Jonas, and two more brothers and a baby sister. All of them — all of them, Margaret — died in a smallpox epidemic within four months of one another. That left Jessie alone at the age of nine with parents who worried themselves into an early grave over her. I thought she was never going to be really happy again, but then when she grew up she married happy-go-lucky Zacharia Muggins. A year later she gave birth to twins. I helped bring them into the world — a healthy boy and girl, just like her and Jonas. She named them Matthew and Martha and she was beside herself with joy. Then an influenza epidemic struck and little Martha sickened and died. Now — can you understand why a woman who has suffered such dreadful loss could go plumb hysterical at the very thought of anything happening to her only child?" She paused, then murmured, as if to herself, "Why the Lord never saw fit to give her another one is more than I can fathom."

"Oh, Aunt Marg ... " Tears were streaming down my face at the thought of all those poor dead children. "I'm sorry. I've never been so sorry in my whole life. I'll go straight down and apologize. Are they still here?"

"Yes, they're still here. Matty can't go outside until his clothes are dry. But the best thing you can do, my girl, until I get that health certificate for you, is to make yourself scarce. I'll apologize for both of us. I've got some crow to eat myself in this affair."

The bed creaked with relief when she stood up. She smoothed out her apron and tucked a strand of red hair into place. "Now you go rinse your face and clean your specs and watch out the window. Isn't it handy that your bedroom looks right out onto the barnyard? You won't miss a thing. And when I've got a minute I'll bring you up a tray fit for a queen."

I sighed with disappointment. And then I asked a

question about something that was bothering me. "Aunt Marg, did you mean that, about being sorry you hit me because I'm not your own?"

"Well, now, I'm sorry as sin that I lost my temper, girl. I've got no use for grownups who beat children. But you *are* my own, Margaret. You're my everything!" Then she hugged me tight, let go suddenly and rushed downstairs.

True to her word, a little while later she brought me up a tray fit for a queen.

I ate hungrily as I watched out the window. I could see Starr teamed up with a dappled grey. Both of them were straining in the harness, working their heads off along with the men.

The framework of the barn had to be constructed on the ground. Then each side was raised up with great long pike poles. All day long the hammering and clammering went on, until the last rafter was nailed to the roof. Uncle Herb would have to finish the inside himself. But at least the hard part was done. It would be a fine barn. Bigger and better than the old one, with a separate stable.

I envied the kids, not only helping, but chasing each other around the barnyard having lots of fun.

Suddenly Matty looked up at my window. I was just about to turn away, ashamed because of what I'd called his mother, when he grinned and waved at me. So I leaned out the window and waved back.

"How does it look from up there?" he shouted.

The last rays of the setting sun glinted on the brand new lumber, tinting it pinky gold. "It's beautiful. I've got a bird's-eye view up here."

"I wish I could come up!" he yelled.

I laughed and nodded and he, reluctantly it seemed to me, went back to join the other kids at play.

Later, when it was too dark to work outside, almost everybody came inside. But I was puzzled about one man who didn't. He was strange looking, tall and skinny, with a scraggly beard and raggedy clothes. As soon as the work was done, he got on his horse without saying a word to anybody and rode off in a cloud of dust.

Soon the house began to rock and ring with the air of a party. I heard loud guffaws and high-pitched squeals, clattering crockery and tinkling glassware.

With a loud sigh I unpacked my grip, stuck the snapshot back up on the looking glass, put on my nightdress, used the chamber pot under the bed so I wouldn't have to go downstairs, and climbed in under my cover.

After a while the door squeaked open and a familiar voice whispered, "Any corkers awake in here?"

Jumping up, I lit the lamp on the washstand. Uncle Herb set a tray beside the lamp. On it was a tall glass of lemonade and a huge slab of angel cake topped with fresh churned ice cream.

"I'm mighty sorry you missed it all, Maggie. But I'm mighty proud of you too. Your aunt says you showed understanding far beyond your years."

"Thanks, Uncle Herb. But don't feel bad. I saw everything from up here and I love the new barn." I took a big gulp of lemonade to wash the cake down. "By the way, Uncle Herb, who was that scruffy-looking man who rode away on a big black horse? Why didn't he come to the party?" I couldn't imagine anybody missing the party on purpose.

Uncle Herb scratched his head with his thumbnail. "Oh, you must be referrin' to old Joe Boyle. He's a funny fella, that one, Maggie. A regular old recluse. He lives all by hisself in the bush. Got no friends or folks that I ever heard tell of. And don't have nothing to do with nobody. But, by George, he never misses a barn raising."

Then I asked him a more worrisome question. "What will Starr and Flora and Fauna eat this winter now that the hay's all gone? It's too late to harvest more, isn't it?"

"Way too late," he agreed, jiggling the straw between his teeth. He did this to help him break the tobacco-chewing habit, which Aunt Marg detested. "But our neighbours will see us through. You can bank on that. Everybody will bring a bale of hay or a bushel of oats or whatever they can spare."

"Will you have to pay them all?"

"Not a penny. That's how farm folk operate. We stick together in times of trouble. Not like city folk — present company excepted, of course." He patted my cheek affectionately. "Your aunt tells me you were as much help as a growed woman this past week, Maggie."

"It was fun. I really think it's swell how farm folk stick together. In fact, I think that's what I'm going to be when I grow up — a farmer, just like you."

"Well" — he twirled the straw around in thoughtful circles — "If I had my druthers" (Aunt

Marg would have a fit if she heard him use that word. She said he was an educated man and ought to know better. Hadn't he graduated at the top of his class from Senior Fourth?), "I'd druther see you become a vet. That way you can live in the country, but never have a barn to burn. Now that's what I call eating your cake and having it too."

"Swell! And I'll have my animal hospital right near here so I can look after Starr and Flora and Fauna myself. And I'll never charge you a penny, Uncle Herb. Not a penny."

"Well, by gingoes, that's the best offer I've had all day." He leaned down and gave me a little whisker rub. "I'm a lucky man, Maggie. I must have been born with a silver spoon in my mouth."

6
A day in town

The next Saturday morning Aunt Marg and I went to Shelburne in the buggy to get a health certificate for me and to do some shopping. Uncle Herb stayed home to finish the new barn.

"Can I drive?" I begged, as Aunt Marg was backing Starr between the buggy shafts.

"Part ways. But when we get near town I'll have to take over because there'll be automobiles to contend with and they scare the daylights out of Starr."

Climbing into the driver's seat, I took up the reins and waited until Aunt Marg got settled beside me. She was wearing her second-best dress and a wide-brimmed, flowered hat held on by two sharp hat pins piercing her thick red bun. I clicked my tongue and Starr twitched his ears and started off at a nice easy trot.

It was a lovely day. The leaves were changing colours, the air was fresh and crisp, and the sky was a brilliant blue. Starr seemed to be enjoying the outing. Every time I said his name he pricked up his velvety ears and swished his tawny tail across our feet like a feather duster. I'd trimmed the singed part off his tail, so it looked full and beautiful again.

Just outside town Aunt Marg and I changed places. Seeing houses and shops and people and horses and cars got me all excited. I had been isolated on the farm for such a long time, and having been born and raised in Toronto, I really missed the noises of the city. My father called Shelburne a one-horse town, but after the wide open spaces of the countryside it seemed almost like a real city to me.

The waiting room of the Main Street Clinic was filled with people with broken legs and bandaged heads and crying babies, but we didn't have to wait long because Doctor Tom had made me an appointment.

First I had to stand in front of a machine that took pictures of my insides. Next I had to go down a long hall to a toilet and wet in a bottle. (That was embarrassing, bringing back the bottle.) Then a nurse, who seemed very nice, said, "This won't hurt a bit, honey," and jabbed my thumb with a needle that hurt like the dickens. "What's that for?" I asked curiously as she dabbed my blood on paper. "It's to see if you're anemic."

"What's that mean?" I watched, fascinated, as she compared the colour of my blood with red splotches on another paper until she matched it up exactly.

"It means weak blood. But don't worry. If you have it, an iron tonic will fix you up in no time."

I wasn't worried because I was already taking a tablespoon of Aunt Marg's herbal blood tonic every day and I felt strong as a horse.

After that we had to wait while the doctors tested everything. Aunt Marg started chatting to a lady she knew — she knew just about everybody in Shelburne — so I wandered around the room reading the doctors' diplomas on the walls and imagining my name on a veterinarian's diploma. Pushing my glasses up the freckled bridge of my nose, I leaned closer, trying to read the Latin words. The lady with Aunt Marg must have thought I was hard of hearing, because she said in a loud whisper, "She's not a pretty child, is she?"

"No," agreed Aunt Marg coldly, "she's beautiful!" Then she got up in a huff and moved to the other side of the room. The woman turned beet red and didn't know which way to look. I was just about to put in my two cents worth when I caught my aunt's eye and decided to hold my tongue.

At last we were out on the street again, grinning from ear to ear. I wasn't anemic, and the four doctors in the clinic agreed with Doctor Tom that I was completely cured.

"Just wait 'til I show Jessie Muggins this!" beamed Aunt Marg, waving my health certificate triumphantly. Then she rolled it up and put it at the bottom of her straw satchel.

"All right, old sweetheart, let's go shopping."

Grabbing my arm, Aunt Marg pulled me across the busy street, dodging between a pickup truck and a Model T Ford that were stirring up the dust at about ten miles an hour. Aunt Marg didn't get to town very often, and when she did Uncle Herb said she was like a kid let loose in a candy store.

We had left Starr at the blacksmith's shop to get him shod, so we had the afternoon to ourselves.

"Does it hurt horses to have shoes nailed to their feet?" I asked, wincing at the imagined pain.

"Not if the smithy's worth his salt. And there's none better than Wilbur Shankley, that's for sure. The Shankleys have been smithies in Shelburne for five generations, so they should know what they're doing."

We stopped in front of the drygoods store to admire the new fall material. "I'll tell you a secret about Wilbur Shankley if you promise to keep it under your hat, Margaret," my aunt said, her eyes twinkling.

"Oh, I promise. Cross my heart and spit."

"Cross your heart, but don't spit. One spitter in the family is all I can bear."

So I crossed my heart and swallowed the spit and she went on. "Well, Wilbur and I were engaged once, and we had the date set and everything."

"Oh, my gosh! Does Uncle Herb know?"

"Sure. He's the reason I'm not Mrs. Wilbur Shankley this very minute. I met Herb at a barn dance a few weeks after I'd promised my hand to Wilbur, and he swept me right off my feet. We knew we were meant for each other from that very first reel. So we got married on the very day that Wilbur and I had picked. I couldn't see any sense in wasting

38

all my plans. But it made Wilbur furious and I don't think he's forgiven me to this day."

Boy! I could hardly wait to meet Wilbur. (He hadn't been there in the morning when we left Starr.) I was dying to see the person who nearly became my uncle.

Inside the drygoods store, Aunt Marg told me to pick out any material I liked and she'd make me a new dress to go home in. Then she frowned at the thought, squeezed my arm and said, "Never mind what for. Just pick out a nice piece of goods — and hang the expense. I chose red wool with white daisies all over it."

Next we went to the Emporium and bought Uncle Herb new overalls. "Now all we have to do is figure out a way to get him out of the old ones," joked Aunt Marg. "He's starting to look as raggedy as old Joe Boyle." Then she bought me two pair of red socks and two white hair bows to go with my new material.

By this time we were starved, so we jostled our way along the crowded sidewalk to the drugstore and sat on soda-fountain stools. Aunt Marg said I could have anything I liked, so I ordered a banana split and a butterscotch sundae. She had salmon sandwiches and a pot of tea.

"Why, Margaret Wilkinson! Fancy meeting you here!" A fat lady about Aunt Marg's age, wearing a hat with imitation cherries all over it, sat down on the stool beside her. "And who might this be?" She looked me up and down as if I was a heifer.

"This is my namesake, my niece, Margaret Rose

Emerson. Margaret, this is Mrs. Wilbur Shankley."
She gave me a broad sidewise wink. "Margaret has
been staying with Herb and me over the summer, so
we've stuck pretty close to home."

"I heard you had a sick girl on your hands. How is
she now?" (Honestly, you'd think I wasn't even
there!) "Did the sickness leave her with weak eyes?"

"Don't be ridiculous, Bertha. Margaret inherited
shortsightedness from her father's side. And she suits
glasses. Everybody says so." She gave me a fierce,
possessive hug, which helped a lot to keep my saucy
tongue from disgracing her again.

Well, once Bertha Shankley knew I had a clean
bill of health she lost interest in me, thank goodness,
and she proceeded to tell Aunt Marg all the latest
gossip. Aunt Marg had been out of circulation ever
since I came to stay with her. She said nobody wanted
you within a mile of them when you had TB in the
house. So she listened, all ears, to Bertha's tales
about who had died lately and who had got married
and who had been born. Boring stuff like that. I
started to fidget, so she ordered me a sarsaparilla to
drink.

"Are you going to the Magic Lantern Show at the
Town Hall?" Mrs. Shankley asked as she began
gathering up her things. She consulted a fancy gold
watch that hung on a black ribbon around her roly-
poly neck. "It starts in fifteen minutes."

So off we went to the Magic Lantern Show. The
admission was ten cents for adults and five cents for
children and Aunt Marg said it was worth twice the
price. We saw slides of the Eiffel Tower and the Taj

Mahal and Buckingham Palace and dozens of other exotic places. It was nearly as good as a trip around the world.

By the time we came out into the dazzling sunlight the Town Hall clock was chiming four o'clock. "My, how time flies!" exclaimed Aunt Marg as we hurried along the main street to the blacksmith's shop.

Starr was all shod and harnessed to the buggy, looking none the worse for wear. Wilbur Shankley himself helped us up into our seats and I could tell by the way he looked at Aunt Marg that he still had a soft spot for her. I must admit he was a handsome man: big and brawny, with dark wavy hair and a handlebar mustache. At first it was hard to see how plain, paunchy little Uncle Herb had won out over such competition. But when Wilbur smiled ... I saw. There was no twinkle in his coal-black eyes and no tenderness about his thin, pale lips.

I guess Aunt Marg knew what she was doing.

We were late getting away, so Aunt Marg cracked the whip above Starr's back and he took off at a trot.

About a quarter mile from home, we stopped in at the Four Corners Post Office.

"You stay right where you are, Margaret." Aunt Marg handed me the reins and hopped down, so I moved over to the driver's seat.

"Be back in two shakes of a lamb's tail," she said, disappearing into the Post Office.

When we were alone I said, "It's me, Starr. Did you have a nice day? I hope it didn't hurt to get your

41

new shoes on." He twitched his ears and switched his tail and answered, "Nicker, nicker, nicker." He understood me, all right.

Aunt Marg came hurrying out, ripping open a letter. She hopped up beside me, not seeming to notice that I had taken her place, so I clicked my tongue and Starr trotted off towards home.

"Oh, for mercy sakes!" exclaimed Aunt Marg as she read. "Oh, my stars!" she declared on the second page. By the third page she was really upset. "Oh, good gracious me, what a terrible shame. How in the world will poor Nell ever manage?"

Fear clutched my heart. Nell was my mother's name.

"Is something wrong at home?" All those exclamations had me worried sick.

"Oh, Margaret, child, I'm sorry. I didn't mean to alarm you. Well, the letter's from your mother and she says Olive and Elmer and the twins all have diphtheria, and the whole house is in quarantine for dear knows how long until they see if any of the rest come down with it. No one is allowed in or out except your father to go to work. Well, that settles it, old sweetheart, you can't go home for a spell. Your uncle will be tickled pink when we tell him, but how do you feel about it, Margaret? Are you homesick, child? Four months is a long time for a girl to be separated from her mother."

I was quiet for a minute, thinking, and watching Starr's brown haunches moving rhythmically. Then I said, "I do get homesick sometimes, Aunt Marg, and I do miss my ma ... and I feel awful about everybody being sick, but" — I hoped what I was going to say wouldn't sound too disloyal to my family — "I really love it here with you and Uncle Herb."

We were on our way up the long lane to the farmhouse. Uncle Herb was waving his red hanky from the porch. Suddenly Starr broke into a canter.

"Well, girl, it's like I always say," Aunt Marg hung onto her hat, her green eyes brightly fixed on home. "It's an ill wind that blows nobody any good."

7

Four Corners School

"Well, Margaret, we can't put it off any longer or we'll have the truant officer at our door. You'll have to start school on Monday."

Saturday was a nice warm day, so Aunt Marg and I took advantage of it by washing our hair in rainwater from the barrel under the eavestrough, and sitting out on the bench in the sun to let it dry.

Aunt Marg's hair was a sight to see when it was freshly washed. It draped around her shoulders and rippled down her back like a shiny brass curtain.

She had cut my hair fairly short, and as she was rubbing it dry, she exclaimed, "Glory be, Margaret, your hair is coming in all wavy at the roots. If I wind it around my finger and you sit still until it dries, you'll have a headful of ringlets, just like you did before you took sick. Won't that be grand?"

Boy, was I glad! My dark curly hair, which I had inherited from my father, along with my freckles and nearsightedness, was my only claim to beauty and I had been broken-hearted when I thought I'd lost it.

I got up bright and early Monday morning and decked myself out in my new red dress and white hair bow. Aunt Marg had been looking forward to starting me off at school, but during the night she had come down with a sick headache so Uncle Herb had to do the honours.

I was nervous as a cat. I didn't know any of the kids at Four Corners except Matty Muggins. Mrs. Muggins had let Matty come over three times and I had been to their place twice since she saw my health certificate and was finally convinced that I wasn't germy. We had hit it off right away, Matty and me. But I hadn't gotten to know any of the other kids yet.

It was less than a quarter mile down the road to the little one-room schoolhouse, but Uncle Herb harnessed Starr to the buggy because it had turned cold and windy. Aunt Marg was afraid I'd catch my death if I walked, and Uncle Herb said I might as well start out in style.

We were late arriving, and the yard was deserted, so Uncle Herb knocked on the windowless schoolhouse door. After what seemed like ages, the schoolmistress opened it.

My heart sank when I saw her. She had a stern face with long, narrow lines that pulled her lips down at the corners. Her eyes were cold and dark, like the black beads in Aunt Marg's button box.

Removing his hat like a gentleman, Uncle Herb introduced me. "This here is your new pupil, Margaret Rose Emerson. Maggie, say how-de-do to Miss Maggotty."

"Hmmph!" snorted the teacher before I had a

chance to speak. Her beady eyes darted a glance over the top of her spectacles to the big round clock on the wall. "Not only a whole month late, but ten minutes tardy the first day!"

Uncle Herb stiffened and tightened his grip on my shoulder. "The missus took sick in the night, Matilda, or we'd have been here on time. It's not the girl's fault, so don't you go blaming her or you'll have me to reckon with."

Jamming his hat back on his head, he said to me, "I'll pick you up at four o'clock sharp, Maggie." Then he left.

It was a bad start for me. Not only had Uncle Herb defied Miss Maggotty's authority in front of the whole class, but he had spilled the beans about her real name, too. I found out later that she always signed the report cards *Millicent* instead of *Matilda*.

"Oscar Ogilvey, move over and make room for her royal highness," she said with a twisted smile. The big, awkward boy sitting on the front bench right under her narrow nose glared at me and shuffled over. Wordlessly she pointed, and I took his place.

"What class were you in last year, miss?" she snapped the question out sarcastically.

"Junior Third," I answered promptly.

"Junior Third, *Miss Maggotty!*" she barked.

"Junior Third, Miss Maggotty!" I parroted.

"Very well, Miss Smarty, you can stay in Junior Third, since you've missed a whole month of schooling already."

"Oh, no! I passed with honours last year. And I'm very smart. I can catch up easy!"

"Easily!" She caught my mistake gleefully.

"Easily," I agreed.

The class snickered and she grinned her appreciation. "Very well, Miss Smarty, we'll test you out and see."

"Miss Maggotty," my stomach was in knots, but I had to say it, "my name is Miss Emerson. Margaret Rose Emerson."

The class roared this time and she silenced them with a loud crack of the yardstick over her desk. I had won that round, but I could tell by the expression on her mean old face that I'd probably regret it.

While the other kids had recesses and lunch hour, I spent the time doing tests. They were all as easy as pie. During the afternoon I saw Miss Maggotty marking them, so at the end of the day I asked, in as polite a voice as I could muster, "Miss Maggotty, may I please go into Senior Third tomorrow?" I was sure I had passed all the tests.

"You will remain where you are until I deem otherwise," she answered smugly.

Uncle Herb and Starr arrived at four o'clock on the dot. Boy, was I glad to see them.

"How did it go, Maggie?" Uncle Herb asked, handing me the reins.

"I don't know, Uncle Herb." I clicked my tongue and Starr twitched his ears and started off at a brisk trot. I was both mad and bewildered about my first day at school. "Miss Maggotty gave me tests to see if I'm ready for Senior Third, and I'm sure I am. But she wouldn't tell me anything. And I know she doesn't like me."

"We'll see about that," he answered gruffly, spitting a long stream of tobacco juice into the bushes at the side of the road. "Matilda's got a grudge against your aunt and me ever since we opposed hiring her ten years ago. I didn't cotton to her then, and I don't cotton to her now, but since we had no young-uns of our own, nothing ever came of it before. You just leave her to me." He let loose another arc of brown juice, trying to get rid of it all before we got home. "How did it go otherwise? Did you make any new friends?"

"No. I didn't have time. Matty talked to me for a minute. But I had to stay in both recesses and lunch hour. I ate my sandwich while I worked. And tonight I have to write a five-hundred-word essay about schools. I think I'll do a comparison."

After supper Aunt Marg and I sat writing at the kitchen table in the circle of yellow lamplight. She let me use the best pen. I was doing my essay and she was writing in her personal diary. We both dipped from the same ink pot.

"Can I see your diary, Aunt Marg?" I asked curiously. I couldn't imagine what she found to put in it every night.

"Oh, pshaw, Margaret. It won't be half as interesting as what you're doing. Besides, it's not a diary, it's just a journal. But I'll let you read what I wrote if you'll let me read what you wrote."

Aunt Marg's entry for the day read: *Oct. 2, 1925. Our Margaret started school today. Herb had to take her because I had a sick headache. My, I was disappointed! I only hope Matilda Maggotty realizes what a gem our Margaret is. I've always found the woman a bit dim, myself, so I'll have to keep a sharp lookout in that direction. It rained in the afternoon. Then the sun broke through and my headache cleared up so I sawed some wood and stacked it along the east wall of the woodshed. Hard to believe winter's nearly upon us. Herb will have to get busy and chop down that dead elm. That'll provide plenty of firewood 'til spring. It would be nice if Margaret could stay all winter. She's such a blessing. Herb thinks the sun rises and sets on her.*

We exchanged books and our eyes met between the lamps.

"Your essay is fine, Margaret," Aunt Marg said.

"Yours too," I said.

"How about some hot cocoa before we turn in?" suggested Uncle Herb, pulling off the earphones of his new crystal set.

"Can I listen while I wait for cocoa, Uncle Herb?" I loved to hear the faraway places drifting in and out on the radio. Two nights ago I had heard Al Jolson singing, "Mammy!" It almost made me cry.

"They just signed off the air, Maggie. I wish you'd spoke up sooner. I had WIP in Philadelphia as clear as a cowbell."

"That would have been a sight more enlightening than my dull old journal," said Aunt Marg, stirring cocoa and sugar into a smooth paste before she added it to the hot milk on the stove.

"Oh, no it wouldn't, Aunt Marg. I loved your journal."

"Go on with you," she laughed, setting the hot

cups down and pinching my cheek with warm fingers. "Anyways ... you're partial."

No wonder! I only hoped Miss Maggotty would be a bit partial to me. I had worked hard on my essay and I hoped it would be my ticket into Senior Third.

8
The switch

The next morning, realizing that I hadn't played a trick on Uncle Herb for at least a week, I thought up a good one.

"Aunt Marg, will you slice my egg exactly in half?"

She knew how to do it perfectly. Then I scraped the hard-boiled centre out onto my plate and put the two empty half-shells, round side up, in two egg cups shaped like roosters. Setting them carefully at Uncle Herb's place, I mashed the egg on my plate, saturated it with salt, pepper and butter, and ate it. Aunt Marg waggled her head as she served up the porridge.

Uncle Herb came in from the barn and began washing up. He filled the basin with a dipperful of rainwater and sluiced it noisily over his face and hands. (He stubbornly refused to use the warm water from the cistern at the end of the stove, saying cold water was good for what ailed him. Aunt Marg said stuff and nonsense. It was more likely good for pneumonia.) Reaching for the warm towel that hung over the stove on a bar suspended by wires from the ceiling, he dried himself with satisfied grunting sounds like a happy bear. Finally, he drew his chair to the table.

"Cold out today," he remarked as he brown-sugared his oatmeal. "You'd better dress warm, Maggie."

"I will," I promised, waiting impatiently for him to get to his eggs.

At last he pushed the bowl aside and drew the egg cups towards him. He whacked at one with his knife and the empty shell splintered and flew all over the place. Without batting an eye, he whacked the other one, sending bits of egg shell sailing through the air. Mabel, the cat, who had been dozing on top of the woodpile, yowled and spat and streaked under the stove.

"For two cents," growled Uncle Herb, "I'd make the dad-blamed upstart who et my eggs clean up the whole dad-blamed mess!"

Poker faced, Aunt Marg reached up to the little shelf above the table, took down two pennies and placed them in front of me. Squealing with delight, I ran to the pantry for the corn broom.

"You're a corker, Maggie," grinned Uncle Herb, as Aunt Marg fished two more eggs out of the pot and I swept the little pile of brown shells into the dustpan, "a genuine ten-carat-gold corker!"

"Eighteen!" I cried, smart-alecky, as I raced upstairs to fetch my school bag.

* * *

The minute I entered the classroom I put my essay on

Miss Maggotty's desk. Then I went and sat down on the front bench. Miss Maggotty had moved Oscar Ogilvey. Next to me now was a small, sweet-faced girl by the name of Eva Hocks. (Aunt Marg always referred to Eva as a little wisp of a thing.) I noticed she was having an awful struggle with her arithmetic and I wished I could help her, but I didn't dare.

At recess Eva and I ran for the seesaw. "I hate arithmetic," she sighed, climbing on one end of the board. "I like artwork best, but we hardly ever have it. I just wish I could draw all day long. You're lucky, Marg, that you're so smart. I saw how quick you got your problems solved."

"Sure," I pushed my feet and we started going up and down, "but I can't draw a straight line with a ruler."

That made her laugh. "What are you going to be when you grow up?" she wanted to know.

"A veterinarian." I got all excited at the thought. "I love animals, especially horses. My aunt says I have an affinity for animals. My horse Starr understands every word I say. And — " I almost told her about the secret signal, then I decided not to.

"I know what you mean," Eva agreed. "My cat Belinda is the same way. My mother says dogs and pigs are smarter than cats, but I don't believe it."

The conversation was really getting interesting, and I thought I might tell her about the secret signal after all, when Miss Maggotty appeared at the schoolhouse door clanging the bell. We both got off the seesaw at the same time so as not to dump each other.

The day was almost over before Miss Maggotty

picked up my essay and began reading it. I could hardly wait for her reaction. But when it came you could have knocked me over with a feather.

"*Margaret Emerson!*" She shouted my name so loud the whole class jerked to attention. "Is this ... thing," she flicked the pages disdainfully, "supposed to be amusing?"

"Nooo — " I was completely perplexed.

"*No, Miss Maggotty!*"

"No, Miss Maggotty!"

Needles of hatred darted from her flinty eyes. "I'll teach you not to make a mockery out of me," she snarled. "Nor will I tolerate you poking fun at this fine country school."

"But Miss Maggotty, I didn't mean — "

"Oh, I know what you meant, all right. I recognize sarcasm when I see it. And I see it in every line of this so-called composition. Your petty little jibes don't fool me."

"But Miss Maggotty — "

She raised her hand for silence. Then smiling sweetly at the pupils as they squirmed uncomfortably in their seats, she continued. "I shall read it aloud and let your classmates be your judge."

So, in a silly, sing-songy voice, she began: "Schools: a comparison by Margaret Rose Emerson. I had no idea how different schools could be until I came to stay with my aunt and uncle on the farm. Last year I attended Leslie Street School in Toronto. It is a big, two-storey brick building with many classrooms. In the basement there is a huge coal-burning furnace that heats the whole school. It is attended by a janitor. The water closets are in the basement, which is very convenient in wintertime." The class snickered and Miss Maggotty allowed it — as if she herself had made a clever joke. "In the city school each boy and girl has a separate desk, and each desk has a built-in inkwell and pencil groove. And the desk lid raises up so you can put your books inside.

"You can imagine my surprise the first day I entered Four Corners School and saw the long rows of benches and tables, and the piles of paper and ink pots that we all share.

"Another curiosity to me was the stove in the middle of the room. I was amazed to learn that it was the teacher's duty to arrive early on cold winter days to start the fire, and that the big boys were expected to keep the wood box full, and that all the parents contributed their share to the woodpile outside. But most surprising of all was the fact that all the children, from six to fourteen, were taught their different lessons by the same teacher. How could one teacher do so much? I wondered. She must be very, very — "

Here Miss Maggotty stopped, just when my essay began to praise her. Holding the pages up between her thumb and finger as if they were disgusting, she said icily, "I consider this ... thing ... to be pure trash, and not worth the effort of marking." Then she ripped my composition in half. "Tonight, Miss Smarty, you will write another essay, this time on the meaning of manners and deportment, which seem to have been neglected in your fine city school. And now, as punishment for mocking my name, you will be publicly switched."

"But, Miss Maggotty — " I could hardly believe a

teacher would be so unfair, "if you'll read the rest you'll come to the part about the country school's rich heritage, and the teacher's great responsi — "

Rip! Rip! Rip!

Even as I spoke, she shredded the pages, lifted the stove lid and fed them into the fire. "Go outside and bring me a good, thick switch!" she commanded.

The whole class gasped. The little kids began to cry. Eva Hocks reached out and squeezed my hand. Matty glared daggers at the teacher, and even Oscar Ogilvey looked sorry for me.

I got up, shoved my glasses up the bridge of my nose and walked calmly to the cloakroom. Ignoring my coat, I went out, slamming the door behind me.

I wasn't scared. Being the middle child in a big family makes you pretty tough. But I *was* mortified. And mad! How dare she burn my hard work to a crisp, the old witch!

I was tugging furiously at a stubborn hickory stick when I heard the clop and rattle of a horse and buggy. Turning, I saw that Uncle Herb and Starr had come early.

Leaping down, not bothering to tether Starr, (who never wandered off like dumb horses do), Uncle Herb cried, "Maggie! What in tarnation are you doing? And where's your coat?"

"I have to get a switch to be punished with," I said.

"What for? What did you do?"

I told him, and his tender face hardened like a rock. With a quick twist of the wrist he snapped off the branch, took off his coat and threw it over my shoulders, and marched with me towards the school.

He flung open the door and it banged against the cloakroom wall. Miss Maggotty jumped, and her face went white. A hush fell over the classroom. Then Uncle Herb did the most unexpected thing. He removed his cap, held it flat against his chest and spoke in a very polite voice. "What's all this about, Matilda? Are you putting on a play? Oliver Twist, mebbe? Or David Copperfield? Is it early practice for the Christmas concert?"

"I can explain, Mr. Wilkinson," jabbered the flustered teacher.

"Don't 'mister' me, Matilda. Just you tell me what this switch is for." He zinged it threateningly past her pointy nose. "Is my girl here playing the part of the wicked schoolmarm? Is that it?"

The blood rushed up from under Miss Maggotty's high collar, changing her face from dead white to blotchy red. Her hand shook as she clutched at her throat. "Margaret wrote a particularly scathing criticism of this school," she said breathlessly, "and she mocks my good name at every opportunity. She is a born troublemaker and I do not want her in my classroom."

"Well, now, that's odd," Uncle Herb pulled at his chin, "because the missus herself read that piece last night and was sure it would please you." He turned to face the class. "What do you say, boys and girls, is my girl here a troublemaker? Do you want to see her expelled from your school?"

Even Oscar Ogilvey hollered, "No! No! No!"

Then Uncle Herb snapped the stick with a loud

crack across his knee, and threw it contemptuously into the fire. "One more thing, Matilda, if this youngster catches pneumonia, or even the sniffles, you'll be running the roads looking for a new post, mark my words! Get your coat, Maggie; we're going home."

At the cloakroom door he turned back, as if he had forgotten something. "Oh, by the by, class dismissed!" he bellowed. Bedlam erupted as my classmates made a mad dash for freedom.

Well, I never became one of Miss Maggotty's favourites, but she never picked on me again either. Not even when I deserved it, like the times she belittled Matty.

Matty was smart enough, and he had no trouble with his paperwork, but when it came to answering out loud or writing on the slateboard he got all mixed up. And Miss Maggotty seemed to delight in making him squirm.

For instance, on the slateboard she wrote sixty-nine. "Matthew Muggins, read that number," she commanded.

Matty hesitated, as he always did, then answered haltingly, "Ninety-six?"

It happened every time. For some weird reason that he couldn't explain, Matty saw numbers backwards. But on paper he got his arithmetic perfect nearly every time.

Well, one day when the inspector was visiting, Miss Maggotty wrote forty-eight on the board and asked poor Matty to read it. As usual, he dragged himself to his feet and answered hopelessly, "Eighty-four?"

"There, you see!" Miss Maggotty squeezed her

lips together as if she had just sucked on a lemon. "How can I be expected to teach such a dullard?"

That's when I exploded. Leaping up, I yelled out boldly, "Why don't you ever ask him thirty-three or sixty-six or ninety-nine?"

If looks could kill I'd be dead.

But the inspector, a kindly grandfatherly man with a grey moustache, asked to see some of Matty's written work. He examined it carefully as Miss Maggotty stood nervously by, wringing her hands.

"The girl has a good point," nodded the inspector sagely. "This boy is obviously not stupid. But he requires patience and understanding, not ridicule and shame. Remember the old adage, Miss Maggotty." He pointed an accusing finger at her. "What the pupil hasn't learned, the teacher hasn't taught."

She didn't speak to me for days after that. But she never made a fool of Matty in front of the whole class again either.

Another thing I did that annoyed Miss Maggotty no end was to speak when I wasn't spoken to. I was bored silly in Junior Third and I always had time on my hands, so I listened in on the older children's lessons. Then, if no one could answer her question and I knew the answer perfectly well, I'd forget myself and jump up and rattle it off.

"Thank you very much, Miss Smarty!" she'd say derisively.

That was one thing that her run-in with Uncle Herb hadn't prevented, her calling me "Miss Smarty." But since I deserved it half the time, I decided to ignore it.

In the end my being a smart-aleck paid off. By

Christmas time she was so sick of me getting into mischief from sheer boredom that she promoted me to Senior Third.If she hoped that the new work would keep me busy, she was right.

9

Lost

For a while there was talk of me going home for the holidays. But several ferocious snowstorms in a row made it impossible to get even as far as Shelburne. I wasn't too disappointed because I really wanted to know what Christmas would be like on the farm.

"When are you going out for the tree, Herb?" asked Aunt Marg one still, cold December morning.

Uncle Herb was busy poking a thick, dry log into the stove. Sparks glittered in the air and the fire crackled cosily. Steam rattled the lid of the teakettle. "This looks as good a day as any," he said, moving the kettle to one side.

"Oh, boy! Can I go with you?" I jumped up and flung my arms around him. But they wouldn't reach behind him because he was growing stouter every day. "It's my winter bearfat," he confessed, patting his barrel-shaped stomach.

"Matty's going to ski over for some help with his numbers," I said. "Can he come too?"

"Sure, just so long as he learns his number work

first. Jessie's mighty pleased that you're helping him, Maggie."

"Oh, he's catching on really fast. It's all I can do to stay ahead of him."

Matty came, and we finished the arithmetic in no time flat.

"Mind you get a perfect spruce now, Herb," Aunt Marg said as the three of us bundled up against the cold. "I won't make house-room for a scraggly old pine."

"You're a bossy old cow, Mag Wilkinson," he teased. Then he kissed her just as if they were young. Right in front of Matty, too. Was I ever embarrassed!

It was a bright blue afternoon and we had to squint to keep from getting snow-blinded. Oh, but it was fun, gliding over the sparkling meadow in the cutter behind Starr. He was so glad to be out of the stable that he pranced and snorted like a circus horse. He must have been bored stiff with only Flora and Fauna for company while I was at school.

Deep in the woods, we came to a clearing, and Uncle Herb called, "Whoa, there!" Starr stopped in a flurry of snow. "This is as far as the cutter can go." Uncle Herb dropped the reins on the horse's back and hopped down. "Now let's see what we can find."

We searched all along the edge of the clearing, but we couldn't see a perfect spruce. "I'll have to go into the bush a ways," Uncle Herb said. "You two stay here in the clearing."

"Why can't we go too?" I protested, disappointed.

"We might get separated, that's why. And it's mighty easy to get turned around in these here woods."

"How come you won't get turned around, then?"

"Because I know every inch of my land like the back of my hand," he answered proudly. Then he slung the axe over his shoulder and disappeared into the forest.

Matty and I waited in the cutter. We talked about school and family and friends. I had shown him the picture of my family and rhymed off all their names.

"It must be great fun to have a bunch of brothers and sisters," he said enviously.

"Maybe sometimes." I felt a twinge of homesickness. "But we fight a lot."

"Well, that's better than having nobody to fight with. I hate being an only child."

"I don't. I like it." I had never admitted that before. Not even to myself. But it *was* nice in some ways. Like getting your own way most of the time. And always being the one to finish up the cake. And coming home from school and being listened to. Ma hardly ever had time to listen. She was always too busy bathing babies or refereeing fights or just trying to catch up on all the work that nine children made.

"It's nice being an only child," I said.

Matty shrugged. "I'm freezing," he said. "Let's get down and run around."

There wasn't much room to run around in the clearing, so after talking to Starr and brushing the icicles off his whiskers, we lay on our backs in the snow and stared up at the sky. We could see a patch of blue through the treetops about the size of Uncle Herb's Sunday shirt. Then a white cloud that looked like a woolly lamb floated by.

We both heard it at the same time — a crunch of crisp snow, a crackling of twigs. At first we thought it might be Uncle Herb coming back. But we hadn't even heard the ring of the axe yet. Exchanging jittery glances, we sat up without making a sound. And there she was, not twenty paces away, a lovely brown-eyed doe. She stood stock-still, looking at us. We didn't even breathe. Then Starr began vibrating his lips, making that airy, fluttery sound horses make when they're bored. That frightened the deer and she bounded to the edge of the clearing. There she stopped, her bobbed tail twitching, her luminous eyes gazing over her shoulder.

"Darn!" declared Matty under his breath, "I wish I'd brought my gun."

"Matty Muggins," I whispered, "how could you even think of such a thing?"

"Heck, there's nothing wrong with hunting. And there's sure lots of good eating on that deer." He actually licked his chops like a dog. "Mmmm ... I love venison."

"Well, I love animals," I said as the doe disappeared into the woods. "C'mon, let's see where she goes."

I had only intended to go a short distance, keeping the horse and sleigh in sight. But the deer seemed to be playing peekaboo, tempting us to follow. Every time we thought we'd lost her, we caught a glimpse of her again through the thicket. But, finally, she vanished completely.

"Maybe we should turn back now," I suggested, looking around at the deep, dense bush that blocked out most of the sky. It was getting dark, and colder by the minute. The bitter air went right through the woollen muffler I had wrapped around my face. It stung my lungs with every breath I took. And my glasses were all smustered with frost, so I took them off and put them in my pocket.

I looked around, but I couldn't remember which direction we had come from. The bush was so thick there was almost no snow on the ground and no footprints to follow back to the clearing. "I think we're lost, Matty," I said, my voice quavering.

"Nah! I know this bush like the back of my hand!"

He sounded so sure of himself with Uncle Herb's words coming out of his mouth that I followed him trustingly. A red tassle got torn from my scarf as we pushed our way through the brambles. About fifteen minutes later, breathless and freezing, I found the red tassle again.

"Now you've done it, Matty Muggins!" I shook the ragged tassle in his face. "We're lost and I'm frozen and Uncle Herb will be mad as a hornet!"

"Nah! Your uncle never gets mad," scoffed Matty.

"He does if it's serious. Remember Miss Maggotty and the switch?"

"Yeah ... well ... I musta made a mistake. It's this way." He pointed in the opposite direction. "Don't be scared, Maggie. I'm awful good at directions."

"You better be," I muttered, trudging after him, "And don't call me Maggie anymore."

"Why not? You call me Matty."

"Well ... I'll promise to call you Matt if you promise to call me Marg."

"Promise," he said.

We plodded on, the woods pressing in all around us. Bushes and thorns grabbed at our coat sleeves, and burrs and pine needles stuck to our woollen stockings.

I was about ready to drop when Matty stopped suddenly in his tracks. He turned around and I nearly died when I saw tears in his eyes.

"We're lost," he admitted glumly.

"Well damn you, Matty, I told you so long ago."

"You did it again!" he yelled.

"What?"

"You called me Matty. And you swore, too."

"Oh, shut up! What difference does that make now? Who cares if they put 'Matty' Muggins and 'Maggie' Emerson on our tombstones? And who'll know I swore when they find us stiff as statues?"

"I guess you're right. It won't make no difference." He collapsed on a crumbling log, banging his mitts together. "My fingers have gone all numb," he worried.

"I think my toes have died already." I couldn't even feel them, so I started jumping up and down.

"What'll we do, Marg?" he asked pitifully.

"I don't know. I can't even find the sun."

"We're lost for sure then." Suddenly he burst into sobs. "Oh, my gosh!" he blubbered. "Oh, my golly! This is gonna kill my ma."

I knew he was right about that. Mrs. Muggins *would* die if anything happened to her only child. And it was all my fault. It was my dumb idea to follow the deer in the first place.

Then, like a lamp being lit in a pitch-black room, an idea flashed through my mind. "I'll call Starr!"

"What the heck good will that do? We've been yelling for help for ages and your uncle hasn't come."

"No, but ... I'll tell you a secret. Well, maybe I won't. You just watch and see." So I puckered up and curled my tongue and blew and blew and blew.

"You aren't whistling," Matty said scornfully. "Let me do it." He pulled his mitten off with his teeth, stuck two fingers in his mouth and was just about to blow when I yelled, "*No!* Starr doesn't come for a whistle!" Again I cupped my hands around my mouth and blew with all my might. Matty looked at me as if I was crazy. But I just said, "Shh!" and didn't bother to explain.

I crossed my fingers inside my mittens, and we held our breath for about a minute, then Matt said, "Listen! I think I hear something." Sure enough, a high-pitched whinny came piercing through the trees. Next we heard a crashing of underbrush, and clumps of snow began raining down on our heads. Then a long nose with a white star on it pushed through the thicket. "Starr!" I screeched, lunging at him through the bushes.

Somehow we managed to climb up on his back and get him turned around. I hung onto his thick winter mane and Matt hung onto me, and my brave stallion crashed his way back to the clearing.

Uncle Herb had unharnessed Starr the minute he suspected we were lost. "I knew your best chance was the secret signal," he said in a trembling voice. I think that was the first time Uncle Herb was ever tempted to give me a whipping. But, thank goodness, he was so glad to see us, scratched and bedraggled but safe and sound, that he settled for a good tongue-lashing instead.

The perfect spruce was already spread out on the cutter, so we headed straight for home. Matt unhitched our hero and led him into the stable. I filled his bin with oats and got him fresh water and kissed his nose a dozen times.

"You know, Maggie," Uncle Herb was leaning on the stable half-door, wiggling a straw between his teeth, "since you saved his life in the fire, and now he's saved yours in the forest, that means you belong to each other for better or worse."

"Really?" I held Starr's face between my hands and looked deep into his dark, mysterious eyes. "I love you, boy," I whispered. Down swept his snowy lashes as he nickered softly and nuzzled my neck.

All three of us agreed not to tell Aunt Marg or Mrs. Muggins what had happened. "What *they* don't know, won't hurt *us*," said Uncle Herb wisely.

10
Christmas

Christmas was funny that year. Nice but funny. I had received a parcel from Toronto a few days before and that set me to thinking about home. I missed the hubbub of a houseful of kids getting ready for the big day. And I missed our messily decorated tree. At home on Jones Avenue, we put it up a week early, and all us kids were allowed to throw the trimmings on, willy-nilly. But here on the farm, Christmas was taken more seriously. In fact, so many things happened I completely forgot to hang up my stocking.

It started on Christmas Eve when we went in the cutter to a church service held in the schoolhouse. After the service everybody sang carols, led by Miss Maggotty waving a pointer. Then we schoolchildren put on a play that we had been practising for weeks. I was the leading angel, and Aunt Marg had made me a scintillating costume. I was the hit of the show — at least according to my aunt and uncle. Then we went home to trim the tree.

Uncle Herb had made a sturdy wooden stand, so

our perfect spruce stood perfectly in the corner of the kitchen. (The parlour was too cold.)

Uncle Herb draped the tree with red and green paper garlands, and then Aunt Marg and I tied on the coloured glass balls.

"Here, Margaret." Aunt Marg handed me a box of carefully packed, much used silver-paper icicles. So I started to throw them on willy-nilly like we did at home.

"No! No! No!" she cried, really upset, "you must hang each one individually so that it falls free — like this."

With work-roughened fingertips she daintily hung each glistening strand on the very outside branches. When all the icicles were on, Uncle Herb set up the stepladder and held it steady while I climbed up and fastened the Star of Bethlehem to the topmost branch.

Next — and I'll never forget this part as long as I live — Aunt Marg and Uncle Herb actually attached tiny white birthday candles in little tin sockets to the tip of each branch. And lit them one by one. With matches!

"I'm scared!" I said, backing away, the memory of the burning barn still blazing in my mind.

"Sit yourself down and hold your breath," whispered Uncle Herb. "This is a sight for sore eyes — believe me."

It was. Aunt Marg blew out the lamps and we sat in a row on the day-bed, me between them, mesmerized by the glittering pyramid. "Squint," Uncle Herb said. So I did and the yellow lights merged and shimmered like stars on water.

"Well, Maggie?" he scratched my cheek with his stubbly chin. "Have you ever seen the like of that before?"

"Never!" I let out my breath in a big puff and the candles flickered. Then Aunt Marg got up reluctantly and pinched out each little flame. Taking them off the tree, she meticulously packed them away.

"That's that for another year," she sighed. "I always wonder if it's worth the trouble. Then I always think it is...especially this year with you here, Margaret."

"I only wish I had a picture of it to send home," I said.

"I only wish I had a picture of your face," she lifted my chin gently, "with the reflection of all those tiny lights sparkling like fireflies in your spectacles."

"No camera could do it justice," said Uncle Herb with a catch in his voice.

Aunt Marg relit the lamps, and even without the candles the tree was beautiful with its wide bottom branches spread out on the floor like a skirt.

"Have we got time for hot cocoa?" I asked, shivering from the draft creeping under the door.

"Sure! Only tonight it's hot toddy for us. This is no ordinary night. It's the best Christmas Eve ever." Uncle Herb got the mugs down from the hooks in the pantry and set them on the table.

I had never tasted hot toddy before. It was strange. I had expected to be a bit melancholy on this particular night, especially at bedtime, but the hot toddy made me drowsy and sent me off to sleep before I had time to think about it.

On Christmas morning I woke to find a lumpy

stocking hanging on my bedpost. It was filled with the usual orange and apple and candy and nuts. I jumped out of bed excitedly, not knowing what else to expect. I had slept late (Uncle Herb said hot toddy affected some folks that way) and I could smell bacon and eggs and wood smoke wafting deliciously up the stairwell. So I put my woollen kimono on over my nightdress and hurried down to the kitchen.

Besides the parcels from home, there were other packages under the tree now. One was a long box wrapped in white tissue paper and tied with a red ribbon. Out of the corner of my eye I thought I saw my name on the tag.

Uncle Herb came in, shaking the snow off like a polar bear. "Brrrr!" he shuddered, hanging his coat and cap on a nail and beginning his morning wash. "Well, I gave the animals their extra rations — not that they know it's Christmas." He rubbed his wind-reddened face briskly with the warm towel. "And I'm ready to tie on the feedbag myself now, Mag."

She gave him a poke, as she always did when he called her Mag, then she set a full, steaming plate before him on the oilcloth-covered table.

He looked at it warily, peeking under the eggs, which were done sunny side up, just the way he liked them. "No tricks today, Maggie?" he asked suspiciously.

"Oh, no, Uncle Herb. Not on Christmas Day. That would be sacrilegious."

"You don't say!" he declared.

I ate hurriedly, and when I was done I said, "Can I start now?"

"Sure!" they chorused, drawing their chairs closer to the tree.

The first gift I went for was the big long box. Tearing off the tissue, I found that it was wrapped in newspaper underneath. I tore it off, only to find more wrappings. Layer after layer of newspaper was tied securely with binder twine. My fingers were all thumbs, so Aunt Marg handed me the scissors. At last I came to a big red Eaton's box. I shook it and it rattled mysteriously.

"Mind you don't break it!" warned Uncle Herb.

So I lifted the lid ever so carefully and, lo and behold, the box was full of small stones. "What the heck!" I cried. Then I spotted a note among the pebbles. Opening it, I read: *Maggie Emerson, look instead ... underneath ye olde day-bed.*

Screeching with excitement, I dove under the bed and pulled out the most beautiful pair of snowshoes I'd ever laid eyes on. "Oh, Uncle Herb!" I knew instantly that he had made them himself. "It's the nicest present I ever got in my whole life. But you're a corker, fooling me like that. A dad-blamed, sacrilegious corker!" Jumping up, I kissed his bristly cheek.

"I thought you might need them to get to the barn when the snow comes deep," he explained, giving me a fierce hug. The thought crossed my mind that my own father had never hugged me like that, but of course he had so many children he wouldn't have time. And it was true, what my mother often said — he was a good father, as fathers go.

Next I opened a soft, lumpy parcel from Aunt

Marg. Inside I found a red woollen sweater-coat and a toque and mittens to match. She must have made them after I'd gone to bed at night because I'd never seen a knitting needle in her hand.

I tried the whole outfit on, snowshoes and all. "Gee, thanks, Aunt Marg. Red's my favourite colour." I kissed her smooth round cheek and she kissed me back.

"It suits you to a T, Margaret," she said. "You look ever so nice."

Then I gave them *my* presents. They were completely surprised, because what they didn't know was that every time I got a letter from home there was a shinplaster in it, and I had saved them all, so I had quite a bit of money. I had bought them both new cocoa mugs because I'd noticed their were getting chipped. On Uncle Herb's was printed *To the man I love!* and on Aung Marg's, in gold script, was written *To my other mother.* (I was a little worried about that inscription because I didn't want to be disloyal to my own mother.)

They both ooohhhed and aahhhed for about fifteen minutes, and Aunt Marg kept wiping her eyes and blowing her nose. Then she said, "Margaret, you haven't opened your presents from home."

A wave of guilt washed over me as I undid the forgotten parcels. The first one held a pretty doll with eyes that opened and shut; in the second one I found new clothes — a dress and a petticoat and bloomers. I didn't play with dolls any more, now that I had Starr. And I could tell at a glance that the clothes were too small for me. It gave me a funny turn, realizing that my parents didn't know how big I was now.

To cover up my feelings, I said, "Well, I think I'll go to the barn and give Starr his present now."

"I'll tidy the kitchen while you're gone," Aunt Marg said, jumping up.

I gave Starr the huge red apple I'd been saving for him since October. Then I braided his mane with a blue ribbon and tied his forelock in a bow. He looked beautiful, and as proud as punch of himself.

Back at the house, I volunteered to do the dishes. Aunt Marg had placed the new mugs, with messages conspicuously showing, on the shelf above the table.

I had no sooner got the oilcloth wiped and the dishpan hung up when Uncle Herb came in and plunked down two pullets, still warm, on the middle of the table. He had already plucked them and cut off their heads, thank goodness, so I didn't recognize them. (Even though Aunt Marg's ladies had no names, I knew them all individually.) Aunt Marg cleaned out their insides, saving the giblets for gravy, stuffed them with savoury dressing, tied them together like Siamese twins and popped them into the oven.

"Jessie and Zack and Matty will be here before we know it," she said, bustling about the kitchen. "Be a good scout, Margaret, and go down the root cellar and bring me up a nice rutabaga and some potatoes that haven't started to sprout. Your legs are younger than mine."

Normally I'd do anything willingly for Aunt Marg, but going down into that musty old root cellar was a real test. I went — but not willingly.

Lifting the trap door in the pantry floor, I leaned it against the pots and pans on the wall. Instantly the smell of earth filled my nose. I shone the flashlight down into the deep, dank hole. The wooden ladder glistened with damp. I had to force myself to grasp each mouldy rung as I descended. My secret fear was that the door would suddenly slam shut and I'd be trapped and eaten alive by giant grubs and potato bugs. I'd scream blue murder, of course, but no one would hear me. Not even my loving aunt, who was singing "Joy to the world!" at the top of her lungs in the kitchen.

I filled the basket with potatoes (to heck with looking for sprouts!), grabbed a huge purple turnip and scurried back up the slimy ladder. Sighing with relief, I lowered the trap door. I hadn't even seen an innocent earthworm down there, let alone a giant grub, but just the same I felt all creepy and crawly, so I decided to have a good wash. I got my blue china jug from my washstand and filled it with the nice warm water from the cistern at the end of the stove. Then I took it back upstairs and poured it into my china basin.

I scrubbed myself fast because the room was cold, then I put on my best dress and tied my dark curls back with a white ribbon. Next I looked in the hazy mirror. The silver had worn off the back of it and Aunt Marg said she'd get it re-silvered one of these days. But I could see myself fine in the centre and I couldn't help but think that if it wasn't for my freckles (at least they were lighter in winter) and my thick, wire-rimmed spectacles that kept sliding down my nose (I adjusted them with my forefinger for the umpteenth time) I wouldn't be too bad looking. And

76

at least I was growing. Poor Eva Hocks was still a "little wisp of a thing."

"I think I'll give my new clothes that Ma sent me to Eva Hocks," I told Aunt Marg. "I bet they'll fit her perfect."

"Perfectly," corrected Aunt Marg. (She was a stickler for grammar. Sometimes Uncle Herb's sayings gave her fits.) "That's a nice idea, Margaret. Eva could do with something new. We'll wrap them up for her birthday."

When everything was ready, with the red candles bright against the snow-white tablecloth and the crepe-paper crackers beside each plate, I sat up on the window sill to wait. "By the way, Aunt Marg," she was putting the mince pies on the trammel at the back of the stove to keep them warm, "don't call Matty Matty anymore. He hates it. We have to call him Matt or Matthew from now on."

Aunt Marg's reddish eyebrows flew up and her green eyes twinkled like emeralds. "Have you got that straight, Herbert?" she asked her clean-shaven, spruced-up husband.

"I've got it, Margaret. Big Margaret that is. And what in tarnation do we call you, missy? Little Margaret? Is Maggie going to be taboo all of a sudden?"

"*You* can call me Maggie til the cows come home, Uncle Herb. But nobody else. *Nobody!*"

"Then what, pray tell, must I call you — Miss Emerson?" Aunt Marg did a good imitation of Miss Maggotty.

"How about 'old sweetheart'?" I said. "That's my favourite."

"Right you are, old sweetheart, and if my ears don't deceive me, here comes Master Matthew Muggins now."

We had a swell Christmas with the Muggins family. Matt and I exchanged presents. He gave me a wonderful book about horses. On the cover, in full colour, was a horse that looked enough like Starr to be his twin. "That's a Clydesdale," Matt informed me. "They're a special breed."

"Gee, thanks, Matt. I always knew Starr was special."

I gave Matt a game board with checkers on one side and Snakes and Ladders on the other. I thought the Snakes and Ladders might help him with his numbers, as well as being fun. But I didn't tell him that.

Dinner was delicious. The pullets were done to a golden turn. The pies would melt in your mouth. And after dinner we all snapped our crackers and put on our paper hats and read our fortunes out loud. "There's money in your future!" mine said. (Wow! Did that ever turn out to be prophetic!)

Matt and I played on the game board while the women did the dishes. Mr. Muggins and Uncle Herb tipped their chairs back and sat with their sock-feet on the oven door, patting their stomachs. Mr. Muggins took a packet of Old Plug chewing tobacco from his shirt pocket, cut off a generous chunk and offered it on the point of his knife to Uncle Herb. Uncle Herb darted Aunt Marg a guilty glance. He had promised her on a stack of Bibles that he'd never chew in the house again. But it was a gift — a Christmas gift from a friend — so what in tarnation could he do? He shrugged his shoulders helplessly and accepted the aromatic present. Then, every time one or the other of them lifted the stove lid and sent a brown stream sizzling into the fire Aunt Marg would clamp her hand over her mouth and gag noisily.

Matt and I played ten board games and won five each. Aunt Marg and Mrs. Muggins chatted happily at the table over dozens of cups of tea.

"It's nearly time we were making tracks," said Mr. Muggins, letting his chair down with a thump. "I've got the livestock to see to before bed."

"All right," sighed Mrs. Muggins, getting up reluctantly, "but my, it's been a grand Christmas. And Matt and Margaret are such good children. Never a speck of trouble." She smiled at us approvingly.

We two "good" children darted Uncle Herb a worried look and were relieved when he gave us a sly wink.

"Want to come to the stable and see how I decorated Starr for Christmas?" I asked Matt.

"Sure," he agreed. So we put on our outdoor clothes and headed for the barn.

Starr was thrilled to see us and whinnied his head off.

"How does he look?" I asked, as the vain Clydesdale bobbed his head up and down, making his ribbons dance.

"Like a prize winner at a horse show!" laughed Matt.

We both thanked Starr again for saving our

lives. Then the Muggins family left for home and we stood at the door until their sleigh bells faded into the cold, still night.

We had hot toddy again before turning in. "It's been my best Christmas ever," I told my aunt and uncle as I sipped the steaming drink. "Ours, too, girl," they said. Then we kissed and hugged good night and wished each other "Merry Christmas!" one more time.

Just before climbing into bed I held the snapshot of my family close to the lamplight so I could recognize all their faces. "Merry Christmas!" I whispered as I called them each by name. Then I kissed the image of my mother and father, in the middle of the group, blew out the lamp and climbed into my cosy bed.

Aunt Marg had filled the brown crockery pig with hot water and put it under my covers earlier. I touched it with my cold toes and shivered with delight. I had intended to think about home for a few minutes before I went to sleep. But I dozed off just as the house on Jones Avenue and my family all sitting around the long dining-room table started coming into focus.

11

Old Joe Boyle

I got my snowshoes just in time because between Christmas and New Year's a ton of snow fell. Uncle Herb taught me everything he knew about snowshoeing. Then he said I was on my own.

So I bundled up, laced my snowshoes to my galoshes and headed for the stable.

"Hi, Starr!" I called the minute I got inside. He whinnied and bumped his flanks against the stall, snorting impatiently as I struggled to get my snowshoes off.

"You're getting awfully tatty looking, boy," I said, running my fingers through his tangled, beribboned mane. "I think it's time you had a good going-over."

So I unbraided the ribbon and combed his mane and tail until they were as soft as rabbit's fur. Then I brushed his coat until it shone like a new penny. Next I cleaned the ticks out of his ears, and once again I tried to brush his big yellow teeth. But that's one thing he wouldn't put up with — tooth-brushing. He just rolled his cushiony lips down and clamped them shut, tight as a vise.

"You're a bad boy," I teased.

Batting his long white eyelashes at me like a big flirt, he nipped the toque right off my head and tossed it over into Fauna's stall. Startled, she mooed at us crossly, but Starr just nickered his head off. Talk about a horse laugh! We had more fun than a picnic, him and me.

* * *

On New Year's Day we were invited over to the Muggins' house for dinner.

"Did you remember to bring your snowshoes, Maggie?" asked Uncle Herb. He was pleased as punch that I was so crazy about them.

"Sure," I said. "Matt and me might go for a walk."

"Matt and I," corrected Aunt Marg with a hug. She always did that so as not to hurt my feelings.

The second we turned up their lane we knew something was wrong. They were all standing around out in the cold stomping their feet and looking strangely excited.

"What's the matter, Zack?" called Uncle Herb.

"It's old Joe Boyle!" Mr. Muggins called back.

"He's dead!" yelled Matt. "Mr. Raggett just left here and he said he found old Joe Boyle — "

"Lying outside his shack in the snow," finished Mrs. Muggins, not to be outdone.

"Froze to death?" asked Uncle Herb, astounded.

"No, shot to death!" declared Mr. Muggins.

"Shot!" You'd think Aunt Marg had been shot

herself, the way she screeched. "Who shot him, for mercy sakes?"

"Shot hisself," explained Matt importantly. "Isn't that right, Pa?"

"That's right," confirmed his father. "Shot hisself with his old war pistol. Tom Raggett said he stuck the barrel in his mouth" — he demonstrated with his finger — "and blew the top of his head clean off."

"Brains flew all over the place," cried Matt, flailing his arms in all directions.

"Can we go and see?" I asked, dying to be part of the gory drama, yet shivering at the thought.

"Sakes alive, no!" Aunt Marg dismissed my bloodthirsty request with a disgusted, "Tsk, tsk, tsk!"

"Let's go inside," Mrs. Muggins said, hugging herself. "It's cold enough to freeze a polar bear out here."

Well, we all sat down to the best New Year's dinner I ever ate, but even during the delicious meal we couldn't stop talking about the tragedy.

"How old is ... was ... old Joe Boyle?" I wanted to know. I hadn't gotten a good look at him the day of the barn raising.

"Oh, he wasn't really old," Mr. Muggins said while buttering the crust of his hot apple pie, "maybe forty-odd. But he looked old because of his dirty, scraggly beard and his raggedy clothes."

"He was a regular old hermit, and skinny as a scarecrow," added Matt, copying Mr. Muggins with the butter. I decided to try it myself. It looked heavenly the way it melted and ran around the crispy lumps and bumps.

"No wonder, living alone in that little shack in

the bush, eating jack-rabbits and berries, never talking to a living soul," put in Mrs. Muggins.

"Yep," agreed Uncle Herb, spreading honey on a baking-powder biscuit bursting with steamy plump raisins, "lived like a pauper, he did, though I heard tell he had a fortune hid away someplace on his land."

"Well, we'll soon know about that, Herb," said Mr. Muggins, wiping his greasy chin, "because that rumour has spread like wildfire and there's folks swarming all over his place like flies on a cowflap; and the poor fella not even decently planted yet."

"You mean he's still out there in the snow?" A ghastly picture of pure white snow splattered with blood and brains went flashing through my mind.

"Nope, he's been took away. He's at Weeper's Undertaker's Parlour in Shelburne. Doesn't that name beat all?" Mr. Muggins shook his head and couldn't suppress a smile. Then he continued soberly. "The man's got no family, and no home to be buried from, so I guess you and me better try to get in there and pay our respects, Herb."

"You're quite right, Zack," agreed Aunt Marg. "It would be downright sinful if nobody showed up for the poor soul's send-off."

So they went the day of the funeral, and sure enough they were the only ones there to see old Joe Boyle laid away in a pauper's grave. Everybody else was too busy digging up his property and tearing his shack apart, hunting for his fortune. They even went so far as to chop down trees and poke into squirrels' nests and groundhog holes, disturbing their winter naps. But after a few frantic weeks of searching, without finding a red cent, they all gradually lost interest. All except Matt, that is.

"I think I know where it's hid," he whispered to me one recess.

"Hidden." I was beginning to sound like Aunt Marg. "Where?"

"We'll go over Saturday and look around," was all I could get out of him. "Be ready about noon and I'll pick you up. And bring your snowshoes. We might need them."

Matt arrived on the dot in the sleigh, without the bells, drawn by their black gelding Bill. The Muggins had two horses, Belle and Bill. They were nice, but not nearly as intelligent or beautiful as Starr. Even Matt admitted that. "Starr's one in a million," he said.

Matt had told his mother he was invited to our place and I had told Aunt Marg I was invited to theirs, so, with no questions asked, we headed straight for old Joe Boyle's.

The shack was tucked so tightly in a tangle of trees and vines and bushes, that it couldn't be seen from the road. Matt took the sleigh in as far as it would go, then tied the reins to a sapling. You couldn't trust Bill not to run off. As I said before, he wasn't as smart as Starr.

We didn't need our snowshoes after all because the snow was packed down solid by the tramping of hundreds of anxious feet. But now the place was completely deserted.

The door to the tar-paper shack sagged open, creaking in the winter wind.

"Are we going in there?" I whispered, my spine prickling right up to my hairline. Matt's pale blue eyes grew dark with excitement. "Well, the fortune ain't ... isn't ... in there. But let's go in just for fun."

He crept up and propped the door open with a stick. I was right on his heels.

Inside, the place was a shambles. Broken crockery and furniture, patchy bear hides and chunks of rain-streaked cardboard that had been stripped off the walls — everything was in a heap in the middle of the floor. And on top of the whole mess, lying on its side, was a moth-eaten deer's head with one glass eye missing and the other staring at us eerily. The stove had been knocked over and the stovepipe dangled from the ceiling. There was black soot all over the place.

Suddenly, from underneath the rubble came a creepy whining sound. Matt and I grabbed onto each other. But it was only a scrawny old cat. It hissed at us, then scrambled over the heap and leaped out the broken window.

"Whew!" Matt blew out his breath as if we'd just had a narrow escape. "Let's get out of here!" His face had gone white as a sheet, making his light brown freckles look as dark as mine.

Once outside we both breathed easier.

"C'mon," Matt said. I followed him around behind the shack and down a weedy path. At the end of it stood a lopsided, smelly old outhouse.

"We're not going in *there*, are we?" I gagged, holding my nose.

"We got to," said Matt. "That's where it is."

"The fortune?"

"Yep."

I stopped at the door, pinching my nose, as Matt stepped gingerly inside. The rotting floorboards creaked under his weight.

Kneeling down by the hole, which was all chewed and splintered by porcupines, Matt turned his head away and gasped, "Ewww! Ahhhh! Ughhh!" He held his breath and his cheeks puffed out like a chipmunk. Thrusting his arm down the hole to the armpit, he began feeling all the way around under the cracked wooden seat. "I feel a ledge in the corner." He let his breath out in a big huff. "Ah! I think I've got it!" He withdrew his arm slowly, and in his hand he held a small, rusty tin box. He shook it over the hole and it made a clinking-clanking sound.

"Don't drop it!" I screeched.

"Shhh! Let's get out of here!"

We hurried to the sleigh, untied the reins and climbed breathlessly into the seat.

"Open it! Open it!" I demanded.

"Oh, no. It's locked!" cried Matt.

"Dammit!" I exploded, then clamped my hand over my mouth because I'd promised Matt I wouldn't swear any more.

"Dammit!" he agreed. "If only I had something to pry it open with."

"I know what!" I jumped down, ran to the shack, picked up a knife I'd noticed in the rubbish and ran back to give it to Matt. "How's this?"

"Swell!" He began prying all around the rusty lid. He worked and worked until the sweat stood out on his forehead. Then, *ping!* the lock broke and the lid flew open.

Suddenly our eyes were dazzled by a mass of silver coins sparkling like diamonds in the winter sun.

"Oh, boy, we're rich! My Christmas cracker was right!"

"Shhh!" Matt's eyes darted around as if the woods had ears. Shoving the box under my feet, he took up the reins and slapped Bill on the back. The horse took off at a gallop. I had to press my feet down hard to hold the jingling box steady on the floor.

When we were safely out on the road again, headed towards home, I said, "How did you know where to look, Matt?"

"Ho, Bill!" he slowed the horse down to a trot. "Well, one day I was out hunting jack-rabbits when I saw old Joe Boyle going down the path to his out-house. I ducked behind a gooseberry bush because Pa always said you could never tell what old Joe Boyle might do. He'd likely shoot first and ask questions later. But this day he wasn't carrying a gun, just some kind of a box. He went in the dumphouse and I hung around until he came out. I noticed right away that he wasn't carrying the box 'cause his hands were swinging at his sides. I forgot all about it until the other day. Then I put two and two together."

"Hey, you're getting good at arithmetic," I teased. Then I said seriously, "The money's yours, then, Matt."

"Nope," he shook his head. "It's ours, Maggie, because I wouldn't have come here alone. And I don't trust nobody else. You won't tell Eva Hocks or any of the other kids at school, will you?"

"Cross my heart," I promised. That was twice he'd called me Maggie since we'd made our pledge. But I let him get away with it because I was pleased by his faith in me. Then I had a disturbing thought. "What the heck will we tell our folks?"

"I was wondering that, too. I guess we got to tell them the truth, because if we don't, and we hide the money, it'll be like stealing."

First we went to Matt's house. He told his mother and she went running to the barn to tell his father, then all four of us hopped into the sleigh and galloped over to my house. Now it was my turn.

"Great day in the morning!" exclaimed Uncle Herb as I lifted the lid and showed him the glittering treasure.

All four grownups looked perplexed as they passed the box around. None of them seemed to notice the bad smell coming from it. "First off, let's count it," said Uncle Herb.

So Matt poured the silver coins onto the table and I did the counting, first by twos and then by ones. Old Joe Boyle's fortune came to exactly one hundred silver dollars.

"Holy smokes, we're rich!" cried Matt.

"Now, hang on a minute." Uncle Herb scratched his head thoughtfully. "What do you say, Zack?"

Mr. Muggins shrugged uncertainly. "What do you think, Jessie?" he asked his wife.

She turned to her friend, "How do you feel about it, Margaret?"

Matt and I swung our eyes eagerly from one to the other. Then Aunt Marg said, "Doesn't that bush lot where Joe Boyle's been living belong to Delmer Pyatt?"

"That's right!" Mr. Muggins slapped his knee. "Old Joe Boyle was just a squatter — not even a tenant. He never paid a cent of rent, but Del let him stay on because he wasn't doing any harm."

"Then the money rightly belongs to him," said Uncle Herb.

"Heck, no!" cried Matt. "Finders keepers!"

"Yeah!" I loudly agreed. "Finders keepers."

"Well, leave it with me," said Uncle Herb. "I'll go in to Shelburne tomorrow and see Del. He's justice of the peace so he'll know what to do."

So that night Matt and I went to bed sorely disappointed.

The next afternoon Matt and his parents came back, and we all sat around the kitchen anxiously awaiting Uncle Herb's return.

When he finally arrived he kept his face purposely expressionless. But I thought I saw a twinkle in his eye. "Tell us! Tell us!" Matt and I yelled, jumping in circles around him.

"Keep your shirt on till I get my coat off," he said brusquely. Then he hung his coat and hat, with the earmuffs attached, on the back of the stairwell door. He seemed to be moving in slow motion.

At last he spoke, "Well, my friend Delmer Pyatt — Mr. Justice of the Peace to you" here he paused so long I thought I'd burst "said ... finders keepers!"

"Yay!" Matt and I screamed so loud the dishes rattled in the cupboard. "We're rich!"

"Just a dern minute," said Uncle Herb solemnly.

"Holy smokes, what next?" cried Matt.

"The money's yours on one condition. That you two never lie to us again about your whereabouts."

Matt and I glanced at each other guiltily. We'd both completely forgotten about that.

"We promise!" we answered seriously, and we crossed our hearts with a great big X.

12
The invitation

At the beginning of March the cold weather broke, so Uncle Herb and Mr. Muggins decided to go into town for supplies. During the long spell of bad weather we had run out of nearly everything — mash for the hens, oats for Starr and flour and sugar for ourselves.

Aunt Marg had even started churning again. "There's nothing like fresh-churned butter on hot biscuits," she declared, working the paddle of her grandmother's old wooden churn steadily up and down. "But I wouldn't go back to being a dairy maid for all the tea in China. No siree! It took me years to wean that uncle of yours off homemade butter, and I'll be dashed if I'm going to start spoiling him again."

"You're a hard woman, Mag," grinned Uncle Herb as he got ready to leave for Shelburne with a list as long as his arm. He turned to me. "By the way, Maggie, your aunt and me and Matty's parents have been talking it over, and we all agree that the best place for that money you found at old Joe Boyle's would be in the bank for safekeeping."

"Why?" I rejected the idea instantly. "It's perfectly safe where I hid it. I'll bet you can't find it, Uncle Herb."

"Mebbe not," he wagged his wiry red head, "but money don't earn interest for future veterinarians stashed away in a hidey-hole in a horse's stall."

"Uncle Herb! Darn it! How the heck — "

"Watch your tongue, girl." Aunt Marg gave me one of her rare no-nonsense looks. "Besides, your uncle is right. You listen to him."

So, with a loud, disgruntled sigh, I went to the stable on my snowshoes and got my fortune. (Starr snorted his disappointment because I didn't stay.) Matt had to hand over his money, too, and when the two men came back from town they presented us with our bankbooks. Our names and account numbers were neatly written on the cover of each red book and fifty dollars was duly recorded inside. But it didn't look very impressive after having a pile of silver coins to gloat over and run our fingers through.

As a small consolation, Uncle Herb had brought me a long paper of button candies, two large-size blackballs and a little game you shook to see if you could get five tiny green pellets into five tiny red holes. On his way home he had stopped at the Post Office, too. But there was no letter for me. Just a small embossed envelope addressed to "Mr. and Mrs. Herbert Wilkinson and family."

"Mercy, what's this?" puzzled Aunt Marg. Slitting it open, she drew out a gilt-edged card. "Oh, my!" she exclaimed, then she began to read aloud, her voice rising in astonishment. "Miss Matilda Maggotty, Schoolmistress, requests the honour of your presence at her marriage to Mr. Archibald Arbuckle, Farmer. The ceremony to take place at Four Corners Schoolhouse on March 25, 1926, at 4 p.m. Afterwards a reception will be held. R.S.V.P."

"Archie Arbuckle!" Aunt Marg was flabbergasted. "Why, that man's a blatherskite who drinks like a fish."

"Well, *he* sure isn't getting himself any prize package," snorted Uncle Herb, twirling a straw in the space between his teeth. (He was finding it awfully hard not to chaw in wintertime when he wasn't very busy.) "But if anybody can straighten him out, Matilda Maggotty can, I'll say that much for her."

"How in heaven's name did they ever keep their courtship a secret, I wonder?" marvelled Aunt Marg. "I've never known anybody to pull the wool over Jessie Muggins' eyes before. She'll be fit to be tied when she finds out."

"Well, I'll guarantee one thing. They didn't use the telephone," said Uncle Herb with a knowing grin.

We didn't have a telephone on our farm. But the Muggins did. There were nineteen houses all strung together on the same partyline, including Mr. Raggett's where Miss Maggotty was boarding. Every time the bell jangled, no matter whose ring it was (the Muggins' ring was one short and three long), Mrs. Muggins shushed everybody in the room, then she stealthily lifted the receiver. It was her favourite pastime, and the only thing Aunt Marg criticized her for. Matt and I listened in sometimes, too. It was great fun. Some of the things you heard you wouldn't believe.

"Am I invited too?" I asked, feeling left out of the whole affair. I didn't even know Archie Arbuckle.

"Why sure you are. What do you think 'and family' means, old sweetheart?" Aunt Marg gave me a reassuring hug.

While we were putting the supplies away she talked a blue streak. I just listened and sucked on a blackball. Every now and again I'd pop it out of my mouth to see what layer I was on. There were three layers of candy — black, pink and white — before you got to the aniseed in the centre. I liked to bite the seed with my front teeth and let the weird flavour explode inside my mouth.

"I wonder what I could make Matilda for a wedding present," pondered Aunt Marg as she dumped the flour into the bin. "If I've got enough wool handy and I get a move on I might have time to knit her up an afghan."

The wedding turned out to be Four Corners' social event of the year. The weather was fine, and everybody came from miles around, decked out in their Sunday best. Not only had Aunt Marg got the afghan done, but she had managed to make herself and me new dresses, too. Uncle Herb said we both looked nifty in our glad rags.

The snow was too deep yet for buggies and automobiles, so the schoolyard was littered with horses and cutters. Inside, the schoolhouse had been transformed. All the furniture had been shoved back against the walls, except the stove. The deep window sills were decorated with tissue-paper flowers and real spruce boughs. Red and white crepe-paper streamers, twisted like stripes on a barber pole, drooped from corner to corner of the high-raftered ceiling. And in the middle hung a white paper bell that opened like a fan.

Everybody stood near the walls on either side of the room, forming an aisle down the middle of the floor.

Mr. and Mrs. Raggett, who were best man and best lady, stood up at the front with the Reverend Mr. Booth, our itinerant preacher.

The wedding was wonderful. Ernie Paddison, Mr. Arbuckle's best friend, had come all the way from Orangeville to play the wedding march on his harmonica. Then, out from the cloakroom stepped the bride and groom. Everyone gasped as they came arm in arm down the aisle.

Miss Maggotty (as Uncle Herb admitted later) was a sight for sore eyes. She was all gussied up in a white lace gown and she carried a spray of pink silk roses. A white net veil covered her face, making her look almost pretty. And Mr. Arbuckle looked pretty smart too. He wore a grey pinstripe suit, his black hair was slicked down, and his moustache was waxed and pointed at both ends. I thought he was real handsome for a blatherskite.

"Dearly beloved:" A hush fell over the congregation as the ceremony began. Everything went along smoothly until Reverend Booth asked Miss Maggotty if she would promise to love, honour and obey Mr. Arbuckle. Up went her hand, palm forward. The preacher gulped in surprise and his Adam's apple bobbed up over his backwards white collar.

"Stop right there, Reverend!" cried Miss Maggotty in her commanding teacher's voice. "I shall promise to love and honour, but I shall promise to obey no one, least of all Archibald Arbuckle."

The congregation held its breath so as not to miss a word. Then Mr. Arbuckle, seeing the pickle the preacher was in, laughed out loud and came to his rescue. "That's all right by me, Reverend," he said, "if it's all right by you."

Mopping his brow with his hanky, Mr. Booth side-stepped away from the stove. Then he repeated the question, leaving out the objectionable word.

"Well, I'll be flummoxed!" whispered Uncle Herb.

"Shush!" said Aunt Marg.

"'Tain't right, and 'tain't legal," grumbled Mr. Muggins.

"Hush your mouth, Zack!" hissed Mrs. Muggins.

I noticed that all the men were frowning, and the women were smirking behind their hymnals.

Then, right after the "I do's" were said, Miss Maggotty interrupted again. "And another thing, Reverend," she said with the voice of authority. "Archibald here has sworn off drink to me in private, but I want him to swear in front of this whole company. And I want it incorporated into the marriage ceremony."

Well, poor Mr. Booth, you could tell he'd never come up against the likes of Miss Maggotty before. But once again Mr. Arbuckle saved the day. Placing his right hand on the Bible and his left hand over his heart, he looked his bride straight in the eye, through the netting, and solemnly declared, "As part and parcel of this here ritual, and in front of all these friends and folks, I, Archibald Arbuckle, do swear by all that's good and holy that I'll never touch hard cider again, so help me!"

The whole congregation burst into applause, and Mr. Booth promptly pronounced the couple "man and wife." And Miss Maggotty interrupted *again*. "No! No! No Mr. Booth!" She wagged her finger in his face as if he was ten years old. "Not 'man and wife.' Just think how foolish it would sound if you pronounced us 'man and woman.' We already know that, don't we? So, you must use the words 'husband and wife.' That makes a lot more sense, don't you think?"

Well, the poor man was so flustered he didn't know what to think. So, red-faced and sputtering, he finally blurted out, "I pronounce you husband and wife ... wife and husband ... oh, for heaven's sake, kiss the bride."

Almost coyly, Matilda Maggotty lifted her veil. Then Mr. Arbuckle grabbed her and gave her a loud, wet smacker.

No sooner was the ceremony over than everyone threw rice, and Miss Maggotty threw her bouquet, and it was caught by the widow Hocks, who blushed to the roots of her black hair.

After the rice was swept up, refreshments were served: crustless sandwiches, iced tea-cakes and ruby-red punch made by the women from their wild raspberry preserves.

As the newlyweds were being toasted, Matt leaned over and whispered in my ear, "Will you marry me when we grow up, Marg?" I blushed and poked him with my elbow and answered solemnly, "I will if I have time."

Next, Uncle Herb and Mr. Muggins and Ernie Paddison brought out their fiddles and began playing "Turkey in the Straw" to beat the band. Up until then I had no idea that my uncle was a talented musician.

When the dancing began, I shrank back against the wall because I didn't know how to dance. But Matt did. He had been going to barn dances ever since he could walk. "C'mon, Marg." He pulled me onto the floor. "I'll learn you."

"Teach me," I corrected, dragging my feet.

"Yes, Miss Maggotty!" he mimicked, making us both laugh.

Well, dancing turned out to be as easy as falling off a log. Matt said I was a natural.

"I've never had so much fun in my life before," I told Aunt Marg breathlessly between dances.

"I'm glad, Margaret." She smoothed the damp curls off my forehead, then took my steamy glasses from the end of my nose, huffed on them, polished them with her hanky and put them back on my face again. "Why don't you go and tell Miss — Mrs. Arbuckle what you just told me?" she suggested.

"Oh, gosh, Aunt Marg, I don't think I better." I looked across the room at the radiant bride. "She still doesn't like me, you know."

"Try it anyway," urged my aunt, giving me a little shove. So I weaved and ducked my way across the wide board floor.

Miss Maggotty was standing beside her old desk, which was covered with a white tablecloth. On it stood the wedding cake and the punch bowl. She and her new husband were sipping punch from stemmed glasses. At first they didn't notice me because they were busy making goo-goo eyes at each other. (I couldn't believe it — old people like them acting so silly.) Then she saw me and smiled. I was amazed at how nice she looked when she smiled. Even with the netting pulled back. I guess it was true what Aunt Marg said, "There's no such thing as a homely bride."

"Are you having a good time, Margaret?" she asked me nice as you please, just as if I hadn't caused her a speck of trouble all year long.

"Oh, yes, Miss Maggotty — " I clamped my hand over my mouth, embarrassed by my mistake. But her new husband put me at ease with a reassuring wink. "I mean, Mrs. Arbuckle. It's the nicest wedding I've ever been to in my whole life." Which was true because I'd never been to a wedding before.

"Why thank you, Margaret." Miss Maggotty's voice was unusually kind.

Having done my duty, I was about to leave when she touched my shoulder. "Margaret, there's something I want you to know before we part." She took a deep breath as if what she had to say was difficult. "To tell you the truth, as a pupil I've found you a trial" — I hung my head and bit my lip so I wouldn't blurt out something awful to spoil her wedding day — "but as a scholar you're a pure delight. It's a privilege to teach a child as bright and eager as you are." She tilted my chin until our eyes met. "This is my advice to you, my dear. Set your sights high. You can be anything you want to be. *Anything*. You might even become Canada's first woman prime minister some day."

Her praise struck me almost dumb. "Thank you, Miss Maggotty," I managed to say as I backed away, bumping into people.

"What did she say?" asked Matt curiously.

"Oh, nothing." I wasn't ready to share the wonderful prophecy with anybody just yet. Not even Matt. Luckily the music started up again and Ernie Paddison began to call a square dance. "Doe-see-doe-and away we go!" he hollered. "C'mon, Matt." I hauled him onto the floor. "It's my favourite!"

* * *

The next morning, bright and early, I went down to the barn with a bag of oats for Starr. He hadn't had a good feed of oats for ages. We were alone, so I told him all about Miss Maggotty's prediction. He listened attentively, twitching his ears and munching softly. "So you see, Starr, Uncle Herb was right about putting my money in the bank to earn interest. I'm going to need all the money I can get. Gee, I wonder how much money a prime minister needs anyway?"

Tossing his tawny mane in the air, Starr fluttered his lips and blew through his nose, spraying my face with oats. "Eeehhh!" he whinnied. Which sounded like a lot to me.

13
The letter

Two whole months went by before I finally got a letter from home. The last one, from my father, had no money in it. Not even a five-cent jit, let alone a shinplaster.

I had written home twice in the meantime, once to Olive, telling her all about Miss Maggotty's wedding, and once to Josie. In both letters I had enclosed a note to my parents. But I hadn't got any answers from anybody.

Then one day a letter in a thick envelope came for me. It had scribbly writing on it, and I recognized my mother's hand, but it looked as if it had been written in a hurry because her writing was usually neater. The stamp was stuck on crooked, too, and the envelope was addressed upside down.

Ripping it open, I found two letters inside, one for me and one for Aunt Marg. I handed her the pages with her name on them and anxiously unfolded mine. Inside I found a wide snapshot, almost identical to the one stuck up on my washstand mirror.

It was a picture of the whole family, except me, standing on the steps of our house on Jones Avenue. Ma and Pa in the middle, looking a bit older than I remembered. Olive, with her head turned to one side showing her kiss curl. (Aunt Marg said she looked like Clara Bow, the "it" girl.) Elmer, looking handsomer than ever. (Olive always said he was full of himself.) Harry and Jenny, the twins (though they didn't look alike), grown long and gangly. Bobby, the youngest, in a cute sailor suit with buttoned-on pants. I noticed the pants weren't sagging so I guessed he was out of napkins at last; he was wearing rompers in my snapshot upstairs. Davey and Gracie, scrunched together at the edge of the picture in front of the post with our street number on it. Then there was Josie right in the middle.

It was Josie my eyes kept coming back to. In her arms, wrapped in a shawl, she held a tiny baby. All I could see was a teeny face with eyes squeezed shut and miniature fists tucked under its chin. Josie was gazing down at it adoringly. It could have been a doll, for its size, but I knew it was a real live baby.

My heart skipping like a triphammer, I read my letter.

May 21, 1926.
11:30 p.m.

Dear Peggy, (It was the nickname I always got called at home. It sounded strange now because Aunt Marg never used it.)

I hope you will forgive your mother for not writing sooner, but I have been up to my ears in work since the new baby came. Yes, that's right, you have a new sister, two weeks old in this snap, named Patricia. She doesn't have a middle name. Josie named her because I couldn't think of another name and your father said he didn't care if we gave her a number. He must be getting fed up with children because he never said anything that outlandish about the rest of you. Anyway, now that she's here we're all pretty taken with her, even your pa, though he won't admit it yet. Josie is just like a little mother to Patsy. I must say I don't know how I'd ever manage without her.

(The news of the new baby came as a terrible shock to me. And I was filled with rage and jealousy at Josie for claiming her before I even had a chance to see her. It seemed to me I wasn't even a part of the family anymore. In fact, I thought the snapshot looked complete without me. I had to take off my misty spectacles and wipe them, and my eyes, before I could continue reading.)

The older children weren't too pleased about Patsy's arrival. But they are coming around one by one. Elmer, who had his sixteenth birthday yesterday — you must have forgot because no card came from you — well, I caught him peeking into the cradle when he thought no one was looking. And Harry and Jenny take turns holding her. But Olive is just the limit; she won't even look at the dear little soul. She says none of her friends have baby sisters and it's embarrassing. I said fiddlesticks! Just you wait young lady until you get married and have one of your own. Then she says she's never getting married and goes off in a huff. Dear, dear. I don't know what to make of young folks nowadays. But I'm glad to report that Gracie and Davey are fond of her. But poor little Bobby's nose is out of joint and I have to watch he doesn't pinch her.

Anyway, I'm sure you'll like her, Peggy, because she has dark curly hair just like you and your father. Come to think of it, she puts me in mind of you when you were born, if I'm thinking of the right baby. It's hard to remember when you've had so many, but it must have been you because you were the only girl born on Rose Avenue. That's where your middle name comes from. (I'd rather have a number than a street name, I thought resentfully.) I do hope she's not nearsighted like you and your father though because I don't like spectacles on youngsters. But they suit you to a T, Peg, I've always said that. (She probably thinks freckles suit me, too, I thought, wiggling my speckled nose to work my glasses closer to my eyes. They were getting all steamy again and I had to keep swallowing a lump in my throat that hurt.)

In my note to your Aunt Margaret I told her you could stay a while longer. I'm so busy now I could do with one less. But later on you can come home. You're always welcome home, Peg, you know that. It's mighty nice that your aunt and uncle like having you. And I know you're happy there with your friends and Starr. Do you still make a pet of Starr?

Well, love, I must sign off since the baby's

crying. She needs nursing and changing, and then maybe I can catch forty winks myself. Dear, dear, I just get one out of napkins and then there's another one. I told your father plump and plain that she'd better be the last because I'm at my wits' end. I don't have time to comb my hair, and I look like a dying duck in a thunderstorm. Please excuse your cranky old mother for running on. I'm so tuckered out I hardly know what I'm saying.

Lovingly,
Your mother.

I folded the letter and glanced up just in time to catch Aunt Marg's eyes on me. She had handed her letter to Uncle Herb and he was watching me too. The snapshot lay between them on the table.

Uncle Herb was twirling a straw in rapid circles between his teeth, "Well Maggie, it seems like your ma's got her hands full."

"Did you know about the baby?" I snapped.

"Not a word or we would have told you. Are you all right, old sweetheart?" My aunt's eyes were soft and tender.

"Yes. But I don't feel like supper. I'm going to bed."

"I'll keep your supper warm," she said, reaching out to stroke my hair.

Grabbing the picture from the table, I put it in the envelope with my letter and hurried towards the stairwell. I turned just in time to see Uncle Herb about to load up his tea from the sugar bowl. He always used three heaping teaspoonfuls and Aunt Marg worried it would give him diabetes.

"Uncle Herb — "

"What is it, Maggie?"

"Don't put that in your tea. It's not sugar. It's salt. I thought it was a good trick, but it doesn't seem funny any more."

"Corker!" he exclaimed, his voice breaking.

14
Thief!

If I hadn't been lying awake stewing about my mother's letter and the picture, I might not have heard it.

The picture bothered me the most. I had cut out my own face from the old snapshot and pasted it over Josie's in the new one. So now Josie wasn't in the family and I was. But instead of making me feel better, it made me feel worse. As if I'd murdered her or something.

For nights now, thoughts of home had been floating around in my mind: the soft pink baby, my mother knee-deep in soiled napkins, my father coming home from work swinging his lunch pail, the little kids running to meet him, searching the pail for tidbits. All over the room they floated — the faces of my family.

This particular night was warm and balmy. It reminded me of the poem "What Is so Rare as a Day in June?" My bedroom window was open because there were no mosquitoes yet, but Aunt Marg had sprinkled my pillowslip with oil of citronella just in case. Aunt Marg was away for the night in Shelburne, nursing Mrs. Plumb who was very sick with the ague. So Uncle Herb and I were alone.

We had a good time together, sharing the earphones of the crystal set, cheek to cheek. We listened to a ghost story all the way from WPG in Atlantic City. I asked Uncle Herb where on earth that was. He said it was 'way down south in the United States someplace. Then I made the cocoa before we turned in.

Josie's phantom face was just appearing on the ceiling when suddenly, through the open window, I heard a wild, piercing cry that made her vanish instantly. It sounded almost like a human cry — but I knew it was Starr.

Bounding out of bed, I leaned far out the window just as a shadowy figure dragged Starr through the open paddock gate by a rope around his neck. The horse reared and whinnied in outrage.

"Starr! Starr!" I screamed at the top of my lungs. But he didn't hear me over his own frantic cries.

"Uncle Herb! Uncle Herb!" I streaked across the hall, leaped on his bed and began pounding him awake.

"What in tarnation!" he muttered sleepily.

"It's Starr! Somebody's stealing Starr!"

"Corker!" he exclaimed indignantly. "I told you no tricks while your aunt's away and I'm all alone, defenceless."

"It's not a trick. Oh, please, Uncle Herb!"

Finally he believed me and we raced down the

stairs and out the door together, just in time to see the thief disappear down the lane on Starr's back.

"Oh, Uncle Herb, what'll we do?" I started to cry.

"There, there, Maggie. Don't take on." He squeezed my hand reassuringly. "We'll think of something."

His words gave me an idea. I ran like the wind to the gate, clambered to the top and, cupping my hands around my mouth, blew with all my might.

Uncle Herb was standing behind me now. We both held our breath to listen. But the sound of Starr's hooves gradually faded away.

Over and over again I puffed and blew my heart out. I filled my lungs with the warm night air and tried and tried again. I made long, breathy, hissing sounds, the closest I ever came to a real whistle.

"It's no use, Maggie." Uncle Herb patted my back consolingly. "We'll find him in the morning."

"*No!* I'll never give up!"

Again and again I sent the secret signal out into the starry night. But I finally had to stop because I'd run out of air and my throat was as dry as a blotter.

Then we heard something — a faraway whinny and the soft thudding of hooves. As the sounds grew louder, my heart banged in my chest.

Up the road came Starr at a gallop, his wild cry mixed with the bellows of a screaming man. The horse thief bounced crazily on the stallion's back like a puppet on a string. He hung on for dear life until they reached the barnyard. Then Starr whirled and bucked like a rodeo horse and sent his captor sailing over the henhouse.

110

Aunt Marg's ladies, wakened so rudely from their cosy sleep, squawked and clucked their heads off. Even the white rooster started crowing.

"Be careful, Uncle Herb!" I shrieked, as he disappeared behind the henhouse after the horse thief.

Meanwhile, Starr tore around the barnyard in wild confusion, whinnying frantically. "Whoa, Starr! Whoa, Starr!" I screamed. At the sound of my voice he gradually slowed down, and at last he stopped. I ran to him and hugged his frothy muzzle. "There, there, boy," I murmured, stroking him gently, "don't take on ... good horse ... my Starr."

Vibrating his lips the way horses do when they're scared, he sprayed hot air all over my face. The skin on his neck rippled under my fingers. Gradually he calmed down.

Then Uncle Herb reappeared, dragging the horse thief by the legs, face down. He wasn't hurt because he had landed in the manure pile, the wind knocked clean out of him. Pinning the man's arms behind his back, Uncle Herb shouted, "Get the rope from the shed, Maggie!" I did, and in seconds the mangy thief was trussed up like a roasting chicken. Then Uncle Herb hitched Starr to the wagon, threw the blubbering wretch in back like a sack of potatoes and delivered him to the constable at Four Corners.

The next afternoon the Shelburne newspaper sent out a reporter to interview me. "What's this about a secret signal?" he asked curiously.

"If I told *you* it wouldn't be a secret anymore," I answered warily.

He laughed and wrote that into the story. Then

he got his folding camera out of the back seat of his Model T Ford and took my picture, cheek to cheek with Starr. The next day there we were on the front page under the headline: City Girl Foils Horse Thief With Secret Signal!

Uncle Herb bought twenty copies when he went to town to fetch Aunt Marg. (Mrs. Plumb's fever had broken and she was on the mend.)

I was an overnight sensation. Matt was proud as punch of me, and maybe a bit jealous, too. Eva Hocks was thrilled to pieces, and all the other kids at Four Corners School, even the ones that didn't particularly like me, wanted to be my friend. Why, even Miss Maggotty — Mrs. Arbuckle — (who had been allowed by the school board to finish the year even though she was married) acted as pleased as if I was her favourite pupil. "I always knew you were special, Margaret," she beamed.

"What's the secret signal?" the kids all begged to know. But I wouldn't tell. And I darted Matt a warning glance. He clamped his mouth shut tight and pretended to button his lips with his fingers.

Finally the excitement began to die down and the horse thief went to jail — for fifteen years! I felt sorry for him until I remembered that it was my horse he stole!

* * *

On the last day of school we got our report cards and I stood first. Aunt Marg and Uncle Herb were proud as peacocks. But I wasn't surprised. I knew I would.

While all these exciting and wonderful things

were happening to me, I forgot about home and the snapshot. But when it was over and life got back to normal, my heartache started again. And this time it wouldn't go away.

Then Aunt Marg, who was a very knowing person (Uncle Herb said she could read people like a book), spoke to me one day out of a clear blue sky.

"It's time you went home, old sweetheart," she said. And she made all the arrangements.

15
Home again

After a tearful goodbye, I was put on the train at Shelburne. That was fun because I'd never had a ride on a train before, only a streetcar. I sat next to a nice lady with silver marcelled hair, rimless spectacles and a powdered nose. (I decided to ask my pa about rimless spectacles. They didn't look nearly so owlish as mine.) She let me have the window seat.

I was so excited I must have talked her ear off. I told her my name was Margaret Rose Emerson and I had a pet horse named Starr. Then I showed her our picture in the paper (I was taking five copies home) and of course she asked me about the secret signal. I hesitated at first. Then I decided that she could be trusted, so I demonstrated my soundless whistle and she seemed very impressed. Next I told her about Aunt Marg and Uncle Herb and Matt and Eva and Miss Maggotty. I also told her silly things like how I loved to play tricks on my uncle. What sort of tricks? she wanted to know.

"Well, yesterday, for my last supper, Aunt Marg

made my favourite dessert, floating island. She cut green cherries in the shape of trees and planted them on the islands. So I said, 'Look quick, Uncle Herb, a bluebird on the window sill!' And when he jerked his head around I stole his cherry tree and popped it into my mouth. When he realized he had been fooled again he hollered, 'Corker!' That's what he calls me when I play tricks on him. And Aunt Marg calls me 'old sweetheart' just for nothing."

"You're a lucky girl to have such a nice aunt and uncle," said Mrs. Bates (that was her name). "Do you live with them all the time? And why are you making this trip to Toronto all alone?"

Her questions flabbergasted me. Here I was telling her all about myself and I left out the most important part: that I was going home. She probably thought I was an orphan child living on the charity of kind relations. And all the time I had a family of my own.

"Well you see, last summer I had TB and my mother sent me to the farm to get cured. Aunt Marg is my mother's sister, and she's the best practical nurse in the whole country, so my mother thought I'd be better off with her than in a sanitarium."

"And your mother was right, of course, because you look as healthy as a rose-red apple. It sounds to me as if you have two fine families. But when all is said and done, be it ever so humble, there's no place like home, is there, Margaret?"

"East, west, home is best!" I chanted. We laughed companionably and she gave me a stick of spearmint candy.

It seemed like no time at all before we pulled into Union Station in Toronto.

"I've made this trip many times before," said Mrs. Bates, "but never has the time gone so quickly and pleasantly. I hope we meet again soon, dear."

Just then a white-haired man appeared, kissed her on the cheek and picked up her suitcase. "Will you be all right, Margaret?" she asked kindly.

"Yes, thanks. I'm supposed to wait under the clock for my pa."

So they walked with me to the bench under the clock and then they waved goodbye.

I saw my father before he saw me. After such a long time, he looked different, somehow. Almost handsome, in spite of his freckly skin and thick, gold-rimmed glasses and unruly black hair. I couldn't think of the right word to suit him. Maybe it was charm, or personality. Anyway, I was suddenly glad I took after him.

"*Pa!*" I cried, jumping to my feet.

"*Peggy!*" He strode towards me and swept me up, hugging me like he never had before. Then he picked up my grip and we made our way across the crowded floor to Front Street.

The sights and sounds of the city came rushing at me: clanging trolleys, blatting horns, bicycle bells and the policeman in his helmet blowing his piercing whistle. People were bustling every which way like ants on a sand hill.

When we stepped off the Gerrard streetcar, I was surprised to hear foreign languages mixed in with the English. I'd almost forgotten what Toronto was like.

But Jones Avenue hadn't changed a bit. The houses were packed together like sardines in a can; hundreds of kids were milling around playing games like Giant Step and Kick the Can and Cinderella Dressed in Yella. The baker's horse was standing patiently at the curb, or maybe not so patiently, since the heavy iron weight attached to his bit had been dropped at his feet to keep him from bolting. I thought of Starr, my handsome Clydesdale, running free in the meadow most of the livelong day. Boy, he didn't know how lucky he was!

Suddenly a jumble of familiar people came scampering up the street to meet us.

"Peggy! Peggy!" they cried. That name sounded strange to me now. Josie reached me first and threw her arms around me. Instantly I forgave her for stealing the baby. Bobby and Gracie and Davey tugged at my skirt. I dropped to my knees and tried to hug and kiss them all at once. I saw Harry and Jenny and Elmer and Olive waving to me from the verandah.

Then my mother came to the door, wiping her hands on her apron, her red face beaming. *"Ma!"* I raced up the stairs into her embrace. She smelled different from Aunt Marg — like soapsuds instead of hay. Leaning back, she held me at arm's length. "My, but you look fine, Peggy. So strong and big! Not like the poor sick little creature I sent away last summer. And don't you look nice! Is that a new dress?"

"Yes, Ma. Aunt Marg made it for me to come home in."

"Ahhh, she's a good scout, that sister of mine. Well, come in, come in. You'll be wanting to see our Patsy. And I've got your favourite supper baking in the oven. Josie, run up and get the baby. It's her feeding time anyway."

Josie took the long, narrow staircase two stairs at a time. But on her way down she watched her step, carefully cradling the precious pink bundle in her arms.

"Oh," I sighed, reaching out for my brand-new sister. Gently, Josie placed her in my arms.

The baby, a tiny mite with dark sparrow's eyes and downy black curls, took one look at me and yowled her head off. You'd think I'd stuck her with a pin.

"I'd better take her," Josie said anxiously. "See how she stops when I've got her? She knows me."

I knew she didn't mean to hurt my feelings, but a wave of jealousy washed over me. Ma handed Josie the bottle and she began to feed her expertly.

"Never mind, love," Ma said to me. "In a few days' time she'll take to you like a duck takes to water."

"She ought to," put in Pa. "You're alike as two peas in a pod." That made me feel better.

The special supper for my homecoming was macaroni and cheese. Two huge bowls of it. Nobody could make that homey dish quite like my mother. Not even Aunt Marg. The top was crispy orangey brown with little scorched "elbows" poking up all over. The sight and cheesy smell of it made me feel more at home than anything.

We all sat down at the long dining-room table. My father had made two extra leaves for the table so that on special occasions, like Christmas and birthdays, we could all sit down together. So my homecoming must have been considered special.

I sat in the middle on one side where I could see everybody. The little kids were all lined up opposite me on a board stretched between two chairs. They darted me shy little glances. I'd forgotten how cute they were.

All my brothers and sisters had grown and changed, but Olive seemed to have grown right up. And she was the spittin' image of our mother, except for her newfangled wind-blown bob. Ma still wore her hair in the old-fashioned way, parted in the middle and drawn back into a bun. But it was the same bright auburn colour, and they both had beautiful, red-fringed, greeny blue eyes.

"Aunt Marg would say 'Your mother will never be dead while you're alive, girl!'" I told Olive.

"Oh, Peggy," my mother laughed, "you sounded just like Margaret, then. My, how I'd love to have a real visit with her again. We used to be so close when we were young." The memory brought sudden tears to her eyes.

"I brought you a present, Ma!" I decided to change the subject. "You, too, Pa." He didn't hear me so I hollered over the hubbub, "*Pa!*"

"Yes, Peg, what is it?" He was eating hurriedly, as he always did, so he could make his escape to the cellar. He had a private little nook down there, with an easy chair and a mantle radio and an ashtray, tucked between the coal bin and the furnace. No one except Ma was allowed to go there. I remember once sneaking down and switching on the radio. I was just snapping my fingers to the tune of "Barney Google" when Pa caught me and sent me upstairs with a whack.

"I brought you a present." I had bought him a tobacco pouch because I knew he smoked down by the furnace. "I brought everybody a present. Uncle Herb took me to Shelburne to shop and he let me have the reins all the way. He says it's uncanny how Starr understands me. Aunt Marg couldn't come with us because she couldn't leave Mrs. Tom Raggett's ulcerated leg. The warm-milk-and-mouldy-bread poultice had to be changed every fifteen minutes so blood poisoning wouldn't set in, then gangrene, then — "

"Peggy! You're making me sick!" giggled Josie, clapping her hand to her mouth.

"Me, too!" gagged Elmer playfully.

Then all the other kids followed suit. Ma said, "Not at the table, Peg, there's a good girl."

I couldn't for the life of me figure out why they carried on like that, even in fun, because on the farm such a conversation wouldn't even turn a hair.

The macaroni and cheese was delicious, and Ma had given me a crunchy helping right off the top, but I could hardly swallow for the fun and elation of being home again.

After supper, when the little kids had been bedded down, Pa came up from the cellar and we all sat together in the parlour. Josie and Jenny fought to sit beside me on the couch. I had never been that popular at home before. Matt was right about brothers and sisters.

"Tell us about Four Corners," demanded Jenny.

120

"Yeah, and horrible Miss Maggotty," urged Josie.

So I told them everything I could think of, except Miss Maggotty's prediction about my future. I thought that might sound a bit show-offy.

"In one of your letters you mentioned a secret signal between you and Uncle Herb's horse," Olive said, wetting her finger and twisting the kiss curl in front of her ear. "What's that all about?"

So I told them, sort of shyly, about our secret signal.

"Let's hear it then," said Harry, all ears.

So I cupped my hands around my mouth, puckered up my lips and blew and blew and blew.

"I don't think a horse would hear that," said Harry skeptically.

"Naa, especially not from a distance," agreed Elmer.

"Oh, yeah? Well I can prove it!" I ran and got the newspapers out of my grip and handed them around. Their stunned reaction was all I could have hoped for. They stared at me as if I was famous, like Jackie Coogan or somebody.

"I'll have to make a special frame for this," Pa said, proudly holding up the front-page photo.

"And we'll hang it over the sideboard," Ma beamed.

That first night home was a night to remember. I had always shared a bed with Josie and I knew it would be hard getting used to that again. But I didn't expect to have *two* bedmates. Now that there was another baby in the family we were more crowded then ever. But still, it was lots of fun, talking and joking with Josie and Jenny, until Pa yelled at us to settle down. Then they made me sleep in the middle and I didn't hardly get a wink all night. Jenny snored and Josie picked her toes. In her sleep! And there was a steady parade to the bathroom all night long. Then somebody pulled the chain too hard and the water closet wouldn't stop running and somebody else had to get up and jiggle it.

It must have been the middle of the night before I finally dozed off. Then suddenly I was wakened up again by the clatter of the milk wagon coming down our street. Through the open window I could hear the milkman whistling, "Can I sleep in your barn tonight, mister?" as he clanked about a dozen bottles on our front stoop. Then I heard his horse neighing impatiently at the curb. So even though I was thrilled to pieces to be home, the milkman's song and that familiar horsey sound made me a bit homesick for the farm. I drifted off at last and dreamed I was riding Starr bareback through the meadow.

The next day Ma let me sleep in until noon. That night I asked Olive if I could sleep with her if I promised to cling to the edge of the mattress.

"Uh-uh!" She shook her head decisively. "That's the only good thing about being the oldest, having a bed to myself. I do most of the work around here, so I get the bed."

I can't say that I blamed her.

16
Back to normal

In no time at all it seemed like I'd never been away. The turmoil of our big family soon made me feel almost invisible again. And Patsy still hadn't taken to me. Every time I picked her up she howled. So one day I handed her over to Josie and said, "Here, you can have her. I like horses better anyway." Josie was horrified.

I was a bit disappointed in my pa, too. After his big welcoming hug at Union Station, I thought we were going to start a brand new friendship. But soon he seemed to forget about me. Every night he'd come home from work, tired and grumpy, sit down and eat as fast as he could, then head straight for his nook in the cellar. And no wonder. It was so noisy at mealtimes that you couldn't even hear the bevy of flies buzzing around the flysticker hanging over the table.

My mother was loving but distracted. One day when I'd finished my house chores, she said, "Go outdoors, now, Jen, and get some fresh air, there's a good girl." Sometimes she'd even say, "There's a good boy." Half the time she was so rattled she didn't know which one of us was which.

Another thing that bothered me was that my best friend, Flossie Gilmore, had found a new best friend while I was away. Her name was Zelma Speares, and when she learned that I had spent the past year on a farm she would hold her nose when I came near and cry, "Phew! You stink like a horse!" To which I would reply, "Thanks for the compliment." But the old saying, "two's company, three's a crowd," proved to be true. And I was the one left out in the cold. Of course there were lots of kids to make friends with on Jones Avenue, but I didn't seem to hit it off with anybody in particular.

August was half over and the kids were all talking about the Exhibition and how much money they had saved up for it. (I didn't have to worry about that because Uncle Herb had given me a whole dollar.) Then came talk about school: would they like their new teacher, and what would they wear for the first day. That got me to thinking about Four Corners School, and wondering who our new teacher would be — or, rather, *their* new teacher.

I had written Aunt Marg and Uncle Herb a long letter but I hadn't had a reply yet. Then one day Ma yelled up the stairs at me as I was dusting the banisters, "Mail for you, Peg!" (I still wasn't used to that old nickname.) Sliding down the banister, I grabbed the fat envelope out of her hand and ripped it open. It was from Aunt Marg and I practically devoured it.

Green Meadows Farm,
August 16, 1926.

My Dear Margaret,

Well, and how's my old sweetheart? Your uncle and I were tickled pink to get your letter with all the news of the family. We both miss you awfully but we know you are happy with your own folks and that's all that matters to us, your happiness.

I was sorry to hear that your best friend deserted you. However, that's only natural when you were gone so long. And you have such a winsome way with you, Margaret, that you'll make a new friend in jig time, never you fear.

It's a pretty day today here on the farm. This morning I caught sight of a deer with its white flag of truce flying. But we're so busy this time of year that I hardly have time to notice things like that.

I have a bit of bad news that I might as well get off my chest (my heart stopped!), but don't worry, it's not about Starr (it started again). Poor Fauna choked to death on a turnip and there wasn't a blame thing I could do about it. I tried, believe me, because she was the best milk cow we ever had. But you know the old saying, every cloud has a silver lining. Well, Flora dropped a calf last month and we named her Fancy. I'm glad it's a girl-calf because we need the milk more than the meat.

Have you heard from Matthew yet? Jessie

says he talks about you non-stop. But not on the party line, you can bet your boots on that! Your uncle and I are thinking about getting the telephone hooked up, since the poles are already out on the road. And it would be a blessing when there's an emergency, like Fauna. Maybe the vet could have saved her. But there's no use crying over spilt milk. Now that's a queer thing to say over the loss of a cow isn't it? Anyway, if we do get the phone connected I have made myself a solemn promise not to pick up the receiver unless it's our ring. I don't want to become a busybody like Jessie. Bless her, I shouldn't harp about that one little fault. She's the truest friend a woman ever had.

Well, I guess you want some news on Starr. (I thought she'd never get around to him.) He surely misses you, girl. Every time he sees me he blinks those outlandish eyelashes of his and snorts his disappointment. And one day last week that uncle of yours left the gate to the front yard wide open and, besides stomping down all my red hollyhocks, Starr came right up to the kitchen door and scared the daylights out of me. His hooves sounded like thunder and he splintered the porch to pieces so now it needs mending. And that uncle of yours just sat there grinning like a chessie cat and said, "He's looking for our girl. Isn't he a corker!" (I laughed my head off when I read that. I could just picture Starr, his long, star-decorated nose denting the screen, his huge brown eyes peering in at Aunt Marg.)

Well, Miss Maggotty, or I should say, Mrs. Arbuckle — will I ever get used to that — seems to have settled in nicely on their farm. But I hear rumours that she orders Archibald around like a schoolchild. However, your uncle says he's never seen Archie so happy, so that's what counts.

We had a general meeting of the school board and hired a new teacher for the coming year. Her name is Miss M. Nesbitt and she is just sixteen. Now how in the world will a young thing like that ever manage Oscar Ogilvey? It took the likes of Miss Maggotty to handle him.

Anyway, since your room is empty now I suggested to Herb that she might come to board with us. (Oh, no! My room!) Herb said it was all right with him if I wanted company, but she couldn't have your room. (Whew!) So now I'll have to get busy and wallpaper that little chamber at the back where I keep my treadle and odds and ends. I guess I'll have to move those things to the parlour, but it won't look very nice I must say. So your room will be ready for you whenever you come home. For a visit I mean. I know you're home now, but you understand what I'm getting at, girl. It's as if you had two homes. At Green Meadows there'll always be a place for Margaret.

When I heard the new schoolmarm's name was Miss M. Nesbitt I hoped and prayed her given name wasn't Margaret. It would stick in my craw, calling another girl Margaret. But it turned out to be Mary so I was glad of that. I hope she's nice and that she agrees to board with us because I need somebody to talk to and do for. (My heart thumped with jealousy.) But nobody could ever take your place, old sweetheart, never fear.

Your uncle keeps pestering me to hurry up so he can add his two cents worth to the end of this letter. He's not much of a hand at letter writing himself. I told him to hold still because I'm not through yet.

You'll be glad to hear that Mrs. Raggett's leg is all better now. I was afraid for a while that it was going to putrefy. But it seems to be completely healed. There's a scar left, though, actually a hole you could bury your thumb in. I felt bad about that but Sophie said as long as she had her leg she wasn't complaining. Besides she wears her skirts so long it won't show.

Doctor Tom gives me full credit for saving Sophie's leg. He says he couldn't have done better himself. Sophie wouldn't hear of *him* tending her because her trouble was above the knee. Foolish woman! But I insisted he have one quick look to be sure it had healed properly. Poor Sophie, she was so mortified when he lifted her skirt that she hid her face in her hanky.

The tinker came down the road yesterday so I got all my pots and pans mended and my scissors sharpened. Then I helped his wife birth a nine pound boy in their covered wagon. Poor soul!

My ladies aren't laying worth a cent these

days, and with Fauna gone — oh, I feel terrible when I think of her — I haven't any milk or eggs to sell so I'm a little short of cash. Flora took sick and went dry, so we're having to buy our milk from Jessie for the time being. Matt brings it over every day. He's a good boy, Matt is.

Your uncle gets after me and says there's no excuse for being short of money. He says all I have to do is hitch Starr to the buggy and go to the bank in Shelburne. But I told him that I'm saving that money for a certain veterinarian's education. Anyhow, if I get Miss Nesbitt's board it'll take the place of my egg money until those lazy ladies start doing their duty again. And Herb is going to buy one of Zacharia's cows so we'll soon be back in business.

Well, old sweetheart, the lamplight is beginning to flicker so I'll hand the pen over to this impatient uncle of yours and go make us a spot of cocoa before turning in.

Lovingly, Aunt Marg.

(As plain as day I could taste the frothy brown drink. Hot or cold, nobody could make it like Aunt Marg.

The handwriting changed abruptly from neat to messy.)

Hello there, corker! How's my favourite trickster? Tied any shoestrings together lately? (Funny he should ask. I had been tempted to the other night when I caught my pa napping on the couch, but I thought better of it.) I still turn my egg right side up every morning. I ain't too fond

129

of empty eggshells. Well, I just thought I'd let you know I'm taking good care of Starr and not working him too hard. Whenever I mention your name he just about whinnies my lugs off. Here's a big hug from your Uncle Herb. (He had drawn an awkward circle with both our names printed in the middle.)

P.S. I mended your right snowshoe. One of the cords was broke. Just in case you come up for a winter visit.

XXXOOO H.A.W.

The A stood for Alfred. Some of Uncle Herb's men friends called him "Haw" just for fun. But not in front of Aunt Marg. She let them know plump and plain that she had no use for nicknames.

The mention of the snowshoes brought winter pictures flashing through my mind: Starr drawing the sleigh over the crisp white meadow; Matt's hair, light as glass, blowing up over his toque; grey smoke curling from the schoolhouse chimney; Uncle Herb coming in from the barn in a snowstorm looking like a polar bear.

It made me want to laugh and cry all at once.

17
Making friends

A few days later I was slouched on our verandah swing, swaying myself lazily back and forth with the tips of my toes, when a big truck stopped in front of the empty house across the street. I perked right up and went and sat sidesaddle on the railing to watch.

A family was moving into the house and some of the kids were carrying boxes inside. Among them I noticed a girl about my own age who looked exactly the way I had always dreamed of looking. She had long, golden sausage curls, like Mary Pickford, and even at a distance I could tell that her eyes were big and blue. And she wasn't wearing spectacles.

Remembering Aunt Marg's words about making a new friend in no time, I went straight over after supper. The girl happened to be standing on the verandah, knee-deep in empty cartons, looking lost and forlorn.

"Hello!" I said with a big welcoming smile, hoping my winsome personality was showing. "My name is Margaret Rose Emerson. I live over there. What's your name?"

"Shirley Shoemaker." She had a lilting voice and a radiant smile and perfect white teeth and no freckles. "How old are you, Margaret?"

"I'll be twelve next month," I said. "How old are you?"

"I just turned twelve, so we'll both be in Senior Third in September. Is the school far?"

"No. It's just around the corner. We don't have to leave till quarter to nine." I decided this was the wrong time to tell her that I had passed with honours into Junior Fourth.

"Are there any moving-picture houses near here?" was her next question.

"Sure. The Bonita is right on Gerrard Street. It's only a hop, skip and a jump away."

"Let's go to the matinee on Saturday," she suggested.

"That sounds swell," I agreed, thinking that if my pa wouldn't give me a nickel I could always break into Uncle Herb's dollar. That would still leave ninety-five cents for the Ex.

On Saturday we went to see Charlie Chaplin. It was a swell picture. The only trouble was, Shirley couldn't read the dialogue at the bottom of the screen fast enough and I had to read it out loud. That made everybody around us mad and they hissed and booed at us.

Anyhow, that's how Shirley Shoemaker and I became friends. But she wasn't half as much fun as Flossie Gilmore, because she wasn't allowed to run for fear her sausage curls would all fall apart. And she wasn't nearly as interesting as Eva Hocks because she didn't like animals. She got tired of hearing about horses in no time flat. And she'd never even heard tell of a Clydesdale. Eva never got tired of horse talk. And I never got tired of cat talk. When Eva's cat, Belinda, had kittens, I even saw the last one come out. And speaking of friends, nobody could hold a candle to Matt.

But at least I had somebody to play with besides my sisters. They had their own friends and didn't want me hanging around all the time. By this time Shirley knew that I was a year ahead of her in school. At first it made her mad. Then she said, "I guess that's because country schools are easier than city schools. Everybody knows that."

"That must be it," I agreed. About schools, unlike my looks, I was very confident. So I didn't care what she believed as long as it made her feel better. But I couldn't help thinking what a shock she would get if she ever tried pleasing Miss Maggotty.

One day we were coming down Jones Avenue hand in hand, sharing a bag of humbugs, when Flossie Gilmore came running up the street to meet us. "Mind if I join you?" she asked. Then, without waiting for an answer, she grabbed Shirley's other hand and started swinging it. Shirley gave her a humbug from our bag.

"You sure are pretty," Flossie told Shirley, pointedly ignoring me. "So are you!" beamed Shirley.

From then on they were a twosome and they dropped me like a hot potato. "Two's company, three's a crowd," my mother philosophized, as if that explained their treachery.

So that was the end of that friendship. I was beginning to feel jinxed or something when along came Mildred MacIntyre. Mildred was nice, but dumb as a doornail. She actually thought babies came out of doctors' black bags.

"It would smother in there," I told her.

"No it wouldn't, because it doesn't start breathing until the doctor turns it upside down and spanks it," she insisted.

So patiently, thinking I was doing her a favour, I told her all about the birth of Belinda's kittens.

"But they're animals, not people!" she protested, all agog.

"Well, people are animals, too, Mildred. Everything on earth is either animal, vegetable or mineral."

The next day I went to Mildred's house to see if she wanted to come out to play, and when I knocked on the door, it flew open and out rushed Mildred's huge mother. She swooped down on me and boxed my ears before I knew what was happening. "You vulgar girl!" I heard her yell through the ringing in my head. "How dare you tell my innocent child such a pack of lies! Now go away and don't ever come back!"

Stomping back inside, she slammed the door, leaving me rubbing my ears in bewilderment. How come I couldn't seem to keep a friend?

"Peggy!" My mother was calling from across the street, waving something white in her hand.

"Yes, Ma!" Could she have heard already that I was in trouble with Mrs. MacIntyre?

"Guess who's coming?"

"Who?"

"Your Aunt Marg and Uncle Herb!"

My troubles vanished in a twinkling. Taking Mildred's verandah steps in a giant leap, I streaked across Jones Avenue without looking and nearly got run over by a horse.

"You crazy little fool!" bellowed the Eaton's driver, reining in the big black animal, whose churning hooves came so close I felt them brush my shoulder.

"I'm sorry, horse!" I apologized.

"Oh, Peggy!" My mother slapped my bottom, causing me to sting at both ends. "You nearly gave me heart failure. No wonder your Uncle Herb calls you a corker."

18
The visit

The letter said they were due to arrive the very next day and planned on staying two whole nights if we could put them up. So Josie and Jenny and I happily volunteered our bed and said we'd be thrilled to sleep on the carpet in the parlour.

"One of you can use the couch," Ma said, her face flushed with excitement. So it was decided that Josie should get the couch because she picked her toes. Personally, I would have slept sitting up on a kitchen chair to make room for Aunt Marg and Uncle Herb.

After supper I helped my mother clean our bedroom from top to bottom. Not that it needed it, but Ma wanted everything perfect for the favourite sister she hadn't seen for two long years.

"You're a wonderful helpmate, Peggy," she said, as I scrubbed the linoleum on my hands and knees while singing "When You and I Were Young, Maggie!" at the top of my lungs. "No wonder Margaret was so willing to keep you for a whole year."

"Oh, I never did much work on the farm, Ma. Aunt Marg was too afraid of me overdoing it."

"Oh, mercy!" My mother hopped down from the chair in the corner where she had been dusting cobwebs. "I hope I'm not making you overdo." She felt my sweating forehead anxiously.

"Heck, no, Ma. I didn't mean it that way. Don't worry. Doctor Tom says I'm fit as a fiddle. I'm just excited, that's all."

"Well, we're done now anyway and I'm all tuckered out. You must be too, so off to bed with you so you won't be too tired to enjoy their visit."

The next morning after breakfast Ma said, "If I knew what train they'd be on I'd send Elmer and Peggy to meet it. I wish that sister of mine had said."

The words were no sooner out of her mouth than Aunt Marg and Uncle Herb came waltzing in the door. As it turned out, they had driven all the way down in their new Ford pickup. Dropping the grip with a thud, Uncle Herb stretched out his arms. I whooped with joy and threw myself into them, nearly knocking him over.

Then Aunt Marg hugged me tight and whispered, "How's my old sweetheart?" Squeezed between them, I could smell chewing tobacco and lavender and new-mown hay.

They hugged and kissed everybody in turn except Olive and Elmer, who insisted they were too old to be hugged so they shook hands instead.

"Now all you kids skeedaddle out of here." Ma began swooshing her hands as if she was sweeping us out with the broom. "I want to have a good chin-wag with my big sister." She put her arm around her sturdy sister's waist. Seeing them side by side, I noticed how alike they were. Except their hair was a different shade of red and Aunt Marg's skin was smoother. I guess having all us kids had given poor Ma a few extra wrinkles.

"But I want to hear about Starr!" I protested.

"Oh, Starr's as right as rain, Maggie. I'll tell you all about him later," said Uncle Herb.

"And Matt, too?" I hung around the door.

"And Matt, too. Now run along before your mother skins you alive." He jerked his frizzy red head towards the door and gave me a meaningful wink.

I finally got the message. Ma and Aunt Marg needed time alone to catch up on the lost years. So I went with Josie to the playground at the end of the street. She pushed Patsy in our rickety old perambulator and I took Bobby by the hand.

We stayed away from the house for two hours, me pushing Bobby on the swing and Josie jiggling the carriage. By the time we got home Patsy was crying and chewing her fist and Bobby had soaked his drawers.

Ma and Aunt Marg had had a wonderful visit. I never saw Ma look so happy. And when Pa came home he and Uncle Herb got on like a house afire. Pa never once went down to the cellar the whole time they stayed.

Aunt Marg made a big fuss over every last one of us. She said Olive was pretty as a picture and Elmer was as dashing as Doug Fairbanks and Jenny and Harry were the handsomest twins she'd ever laid eyes on. She said Gracie and Davey were cute as a bug's ears and Bobby was a blond charmer. And Patsy ... well, when she held Patsy in her arms and gazed down at her adoringly, I just got sick with jealousy. At that moment I thought I hated the baby. But the next thing Aunt Marg said made all the difference. "Oh, she's beautiful!" she breathed, sticking her little finger through a soft, black ringlet. "Why she's the spittin' image of our Margaret."

Hearing those words put out the jealous fire in me as quick as the wind blows out a candle.

"Who's taking care of the animals, Uncle Herb?" I asked that night when the little kids were all bedded down. The rest of us were sitting around the kitchen table having a repast (as Aunt Marg called it). Of course Uncle Herb knew what animal I was talking about.

"Matthew is tending to everything," he assured me. "Him and Starr get along just dandy."

"And Zack or Jessie could get there in two shakes of a lamb's tail, if need be," put in Aunt Marg, "because we've got the phone in now."

"You have?"

"Yes. And I must say it's nice. I have a chat with Jessie nearly every day. Just a short chat, mind."

"And are you keeping your solemn promise to yourself?" I asked mischievously.

"Absolutely!" she declared self-righteously.

"Well, now, hold the phone." Uncle Herb scratched his whiskery chin, his blue eyes twinkling. "There was one call when you weren't sure whose ring it was, and it took you a mighty long time to figure it out, Mag."

"Herbert Wilkinson, you're a prevaricator!" She thumped him on the head with her wide gold wedding band. "I hung up in an instant. One instant — that's all the time I listened."

Uncle Herb rubbed his damaged head, then we collapsed into each other's arms, laughing uproariously.

"Oh, you two!" Aunt Marg scolded. "You're a pair of corkers if you ask me."

"Eighteen carat?" I squealed hysterically.

"No, ten, and not a speck more," she grinned.

Josie huffed impatiently, and the rest looked on bewildered. They didn't understand our "family" jokes.

The next day we all got up bright and early and went to the Ex. All except Patsy, who stayed with our nextdoor neighbour, Mrs. Murphy.

The first building Uncle Herb wanted to see was the Horse Palace.

"For pity sakes," fussed Aunt Marg, "don't you get enough of those creatures at home?"

"Nope. How about you, Maggie? You coming with your pa and me?"

So I went with the men, and Olive and Elmer had to take the middle kids with them to the midway, and Ma and Aunt Marg took Bobby and headed for the flower show.

The first horse we saw was a Clydesdale. I went straight up to him and was about to walk into his stall when his owner said, "Don't go near him, girlie. He's a kicker."

"Oh, he won't kick me," I replied confidently. "I've got a horse just like him."

Before the owner had a chance to stop me, I sidled

into the stall, murmuring softly in horse talk.

"Well, I'll be — " declared the dumbfounded owner, and Uncle Herb chuckled when the ornery Clydesdale nuzzled my shoulder as if he'd known me all his life.

After the horses, we inspected the cattle. One of the cows had a darling calf and I let it suck my finger. Then I remembered about Fancy and tingled with excitement. I decided I liked calves even better than babies.

Later we all met at the fountain and Uncle Herb insisted on treating the whole bunch of us to supper in the restaurant under the grandstand.

"It'll cost you an arm and a leg," Pa protested. But Uncle Herb wouldn't have it any other way. So we all crowded around one big table and I sat between Uncle Herb and Aunt Marg. I was marvellously happy. Flossie and Zelma and Mildred and Shirley could all go jump in the lake and go under three times and come up twice for all I cared.

We stayed until the Exhibition lights came on and the whole place turned into a fairyland. It was amazing how the day's litter seemed to disappear when the coloured lights of the fountain made rainbows in the sky.

The next day Ma and Aunt Marg packed a huge picnic hamper and the bunch of us headed for Centre Island. This time we took Patsy and she was as good as gold.

Little Bobby was beside himself with excitement over his first ferryboat ride. The only problem was getting him off on the other side of the bay. Pa had to pry his fat little fists from the wire mesh under the railing. Then it took Ma about ten minutes to persuade him to stop his bellyaching because he was going to have another boat ride home.

All us kids, including Olive and Elmer, wore our bathing costumes under our clothes so we could splash in the green water. The grownups sprawled on a blanket under a shady weeping willow.

I guess we were the happiest people on Centre Island that day. Uncle Herb kept saying, "Ain't life grand!" as he twirled a slender spear of green grass between his teeth. Aunt Marg had brought her new Brownie, and every time one of us kids hollered for them to watch, she snapped our picture. "For posterity," she said.

On our way home a full moon was riding in the inky blue sky. Bobby pressed his cheek against the wire mesh, mesmerized by the moonlight dancing in the wavy wake of the *Ned Hanlon*. He fell sound asleep on his knees. When Pa picked him up and laid him on his shoulder, there were crisscross marks on his sunburned cheek.

We were so tired when we got home that all us kids went straight to bed without a whimper. But the grownups sat in the kitchen, relaxing and talking over a cup of tea. The door was open a crack and a beam of yellow light ran along the bottom and up the side of the kitchen door.

I lay on the parlour floor, struggling to stay awake because I didn't want to miss a minute of Aunt Margaret and Uncle Herb's visit. I knew they would be heading home early the next morning.

Josie and Jenny were sleeping noisily, Jenny snoring steadily and Josie pick-pick-picking her toes. I strained my ears to eavesdrop, but all I could hear was quiet whispering, and once I thought I heard my name.

Try as I might, I couldn't stay awake another minute.

19
Saying goodbye

The next morning I was the first kid up and dressed. It was still quite dark, but there was a light underneath the kitchen door.

I opened it quietly and there was Aunt Marg standing at the stove, my mother's apron tied in a blue bow across her broad bottom. She was scrambling new-laid eggs from the farm. My mother was frying bacon alongside her, and their freckled arms were touching as they talked in whispers.

Coffee was perking on the back gas jet. The blue flames made dark streaks up the sides of the white enamel pot. The kitchen smelled as delicious as a restaurant.

Pa and Uncle Herb were sitting at the freshly laid table. Uncle Herb's face was red and shiny from shaving. Pa still had a stubbly black beard.

"Good morning!" I said, my owlish spectacles sliding down my nose. Automatically, I pushed them up again. (Pa hadn't taken to the notion of rimless. They wouldn't suit children, he said.)

When I spoke they all jumped and stopped talking and stared at me as if I was a stranger. Their expressions were so peculiar that I looked down at myself to see if I was buttoned up properly.

"Maybe we better put it to her before the others wake up," Pa said.

"Maybe we ought," agreed Uncle Herb solemnly.

Ma wiped her hands on her apron and turned off the gas.

"What's the matter?" I said. They were making me all jittery, looking at me like that.

"Well now, Peg — " Ma was twisting her apron nervously. "What we've got to say doesn't come easy."

"What have you got to say?" I was getting scareder by the second.

"Well, the four of us had a long talk about you last night ... " there was a strange catch in Pa's voice, "and ... well ... you tell her, Herb."

"Well, it's not my place," said Uncle Herb, twirling an imaginary straw between his teeth.

I was fit to be tied with all their well, well, welling. "What are you talking about? Am I sick again?"

"No, no, no, girl!" Aunt Marg grabbed me to her bosom. "It's nothing like that. But your mother does have something important to say. Now out with it, Nell, plump and plain."

Taking me by the shoulders, my mother turned me gently around. Her green eyes were moist and shiny. She drew in a deep breath. "Peggy," she began, "how would you feel about going to live with your aunt and uncle and being brought up the rest of the way by them?"

My eyes darted from one set of grownups to the

other. "You mean for good, as if I was their own girl?" My voice had gone squeaky and my scalp prickled under my mop of black hair.

"That's right." Pa sounded relieved now that it was out. "They're willing to raise you and educate you better than we ever could. But that don't mean your ma and me don't want you, Peg. Or don't love you like the rest. We only want what's best for you."

"You'd always be welcome home, Peggy," my mother added quickly. "It wouldn't change our feelings."

"Your uncle and I would dearly love to have you, Margaret. And we'd see you got home whenever you had the need. Well, love, what do you say?"

I just stood there dumbstruck.

"Let the girl have time to think it over," my wise uncle said. "The final decision rests with her."

The prickly sensation had spread all over my body. I could feel little hairs standing up on my arms. There wasn't a sound in the kitchen except one last perk from the coffee pot.

I didn't know what to say. The last thing I wanted to do was to hurt my parents' feelings. But the thought of going home with Aunt Marg and Uncle Herb, to Matt and Eva, to Four Corners School, to my own little room in the farmhouse and to Starr! Thrills chased up and down my spine. But I knew I must answer carefully.

Facing my mother, I said, "I'd like to go back to the farm, Ma, because I'm going to be a veterinarian when I grow up, and being around farm animals is good practice. But Ma, Pa, it isn't because I'm not happy here, you know."

146

"We know, dear, we know!" Ma hugged me tearfully and Pa sat biting his lower lip. But they both looked relieved.

Then I thought of something. "By the way, Aunt Marg, is Miss Nesbitt going to live with us?" I tried to sound casual, as if I didn't care one way or the other.

"No, love, she's already settled with the Raggetts. She's going to earn her keep by helping Sophie with the chores. Sophie's leg still acts up when it rains."

Just then Josie came into the room carrying a wet, squalling baby. Pretty soon the whole family had assembled and there was such a hubbub in the kitchen that they didn't find out what was happening until after breakfast. When they were told, they all looked at me curiously, as if they didn't know whether to be envious or sorry.

I tried not to act too excited or in too big a hurry to leave, but my heart was beating like a humming-bird's wings as I packed my grip.

"I'll send the rest of your things by parcel post," Ma said, wringing her hands in agitation.

I looked up from my packing, "Ma, you know that snapshot you sent me of the family, with Josie holding the baby?"

"What about it, Peg?" She started refolding my clothes to keep her hands busy.

"Well, I ruined it by pasting my face over Josie's. I wish I hadn't done that. Can you get me another one?"

"I've got a better idea," said Aunt Marg. She was standing at the bedroom door, her hat already perched on top of her shiny bun. "There's two snaps left in my camera. Why don't I take a family portrait? I'll take two to be sure I get a good one."

So that's what she did. We all lined up according to size on the front steps of our house on Jones Avenue just as the sun came beaming over the housetops on the other side of the street. Josie let me hold Patsy and for once she didn't cry. "Smile, everybody!" called Aunt Marg. And we kept the smiles glued to our faces while she snapped us twice.

Pa started cranking at the front of the truck while Uncle Herb sat in the cab revving up the engine. Everybody kissed everybody goodbye. Then, before we all burst out crying, I climbed into the cab between my aunt and uncle.

As we drove up Jones Avenue, I kept waving out the little back window until the truck turned onto Gerrard Street and my family was lost from sight.

We passed the Bonita and I thought of Shirley and Flossie and Zelma and Mildred. I wished they had seen me leave. I would have liked to thumb my nose at them.

The smell of the upholstery in the new Ford pickup reminded me of the doctor's Pierce Arrow. Boy, was I glad I wasn't sick this trip.

"Whew!" breathed Uncle Herb, the sweat beading on his brow. "This traffic is wilder than a stampede." He wrestled the truck along Gerrard Street. "And these dad-blamed trolley tracks are enough to ruin a man's tires."

Aunt Marg and I grinned and kept quiet.

"*Gee!*" commanded Uncle Herb to the truck as he

made a right turn onto Yonge Street. Then, some time later, he hollered *"Haw!"* as he wheeled the truck left onto the dirt road called Eglinton Avenue.

"Drive faster, Uncle Herb!" The speedometer read only twenty miles an hour and there wasn't another car in sight.

"No siree!" He was relaxing against the seat back, chewing like a contented cow, the city safely behind him. "If the Lord had meant us to fly he'd of given us wings."

"Oh, fiddlesticks!" Aunt Marg grabbed onto her hat. "Get a move on. Our Margaret's in a hurry to get home."

So Uncle Herb speeded up to twenty-five miles an hour, but wild horses wouldn't make him go faster.

Every once in a while he sent a stream of tobacco juice sailing out the window. Sometimes a fine spray blew back in. "Herb Wilkinson!" Aunt Marg scolded, "you promised to stop that filthy habit. Why, there's brown specks all over our girl's face. Stick out your tongue, Margaret." I did, then she wet her hanky on it and scrubbed my cheeks.

"There's specks on my specs too, Aunt Marg," I giggled.

"Oh, pshaw, so there is. Stop it this minute, Herbert!"

"I promised not to chaw in the house, Mag, and this ain't the house. Ain't that right, Maggie?" He winked at me, then added, "Oh, sorry about them specks, but they won't do you a speck of harm."

I shrieked with laughter.

"You're a pair of corkers, both of you," declared Aunt Marg, pretending to be mad, "and not gold corkers either. Just plain tin."

"Oh, boy!" I squealed happily. "This is just like old times!"

Uncle Herb took a back road, skirting Shelburne, so I had no idea how close we were to home. Then, suddenly, like a vision or a mirage, there at the end of the long lane was a bright green farmhouse.

"You painted our house! You painted our house!" I screamed.

"Wait'll you see your bedroom, girl!" beamed Aunt Marg, hugging me.

As we pulled in at the gate I noticed a brand new *Green Meadows* sign nailed to the freshly painted post.

"Matt must have done that to welcome you home," declared Uncle Herb. "It wasn't there when we left."

"How did he know I was coming?"

"A little bird must have told him."

At last he parked the truck in front of the driving shed where our dear old buggy sat idle.

"Hurry up, Aunt Marg. Get out! Get out! I can't wait to step on our farm!"

"Well, mercy me, Margaret, I'm not as young as I used to be, you know." She laughed as she struggled to get her short legs from the running board to the ground. Leaping past her, I ran like a jack-rabbit to the split-rail fence.

Leaning against the top rail, I gazed all around the meadow, but I couldn't see a thing. The field seemed empty.

I filled my lungs, cupped my hands around my mouth, and blew with all my might.

Suddenly, on the far side of the pasture, a brown head shot up and swung in my direction. The big Clydesdale hesitated for a split second, then, with a tossing mane and a piercing whinny, Starr came thundering to welcome me home.

BERNICE THURMAN HUNTER

Bernice Thurman Hunter won the 1990 Vicky Metcalf Award for her contribution to Canadian children's literature. She is best known for her Booky trilogy — stories about growing up during the Great Depression. The first in the series, *That Scatterbrain Booky*, won the 1981 IODE Award, and has been made into a play.

As well as the Margaret series, Bernice has written *Lamplighter*, which paints an authentic picture of life in Northern Ontario during the 1880s, and *The Railroader*, the exciting adventures of a boy in the late 1940s who dreams of becoming a railroad engineer. Her books have been translated into many languages and are read around the world.

Bernice enjoys meeting her readers as she visits schools and libraries across Canada.